Contents

1 Lost in the Storm 5

2 The Curious Kitten 123

3 The Homeless Kitten 247

STRIPES PUBLISHING LIMITED
An imprint of the Little Tiger Group
1 Coda Studios, 189 Munster Road,
London SW6 6AW

A paperback original
First published in Great Britain in 2022

Imported into the EEA by Penguin Random House Ireland,
Morrison Chambers, 32 Nassau Street, Dublin D02 YH68

ISBN: 978-1-78895-425-9

A CIP catalogue record for this book is available from the British Library.

Printed and bound in the UK.

10 9 8 7 6 5 4 3 2 1

Kitten Love

Holly Webb

Illustrated by Sophy Williams

Ot[illegible] y Webb

Lost in the Snow
Alfie all Alone
Lost in the Storm
Sam the Stolen Puppy
Max the Missing Puppy
Sky the Unwanted Kitten
Timmy in Trouble
Ginger the Stray Kitten
Harry the Homeless Puppy
Buttons the Runaway Puppy
Alone in the Night
Ellie the Homesick Puppy
Jess the Lonely Puppy
Misty the Abandoned Kitten
Oscar's Lonely Christmas
Lucy the Poorly Puppy
Smudge the Stolen Kitten
The Rescued Puppy
The Kitten Nobody Wanted
The Lost Puppy
The Frightened Kitten
The Secret Puppy
The Abandoned Puppy
The Missing Kitten
The Puppy who was Left Behind
The Kidnapped Kitten
The Scruffy Puppy
The Brave Kitten
The Forgotten Puppy
The Secret Kitten
A Home for Molly
Sammy the Shy Kitten
The Seaside Puppy
The Curious Kitten
Monty the Sad Puppy
The Homeless Kitten
A Kitten Called Tiger
The Unwanted Puppy
The Rescued Kitten
The Shelter Puppy
The Perfect Kitten
The Puppy Who Couldn't Sleep
The Loneliest Kitten
The Mystery Kitten
The Story Puppy
The Saddest Kitten
The Kitten Next Door
The Puppy Who Ran Away
Nadia and the Forever Kitten
A Puppy's First Christmas
The Homesick Kitten
The Frightened Puppy

Lost in the Storm

For Tom

Chapter One

Fluff the kitten was lying in her basket on her back, showing off her furry tummy and snoring a little. She wasn't deeply asleep, just dozing, with her paws tucked under her chin. Her little body only took up one corner of the basket. Fluff was getting bigger, just not very fast. The basket was in a patch of winter sunshine, and it was deliciously cosy. She was planning to spend as much of the afternoon as possible like this. She needed to keep her energy up, after all, for when Ella got home from school and wanted to play.

Ella's mum walked past, and Fluff opened one eye thoughtfully. Was there any chance of a snack? Ella's mum reached down to tickle her behind the ears. She hadn't wanted Ella to have a cat at first. When she and Ella first met Fluff at the farm where she'd been born, Mum had called Fluff a dirty, scruffy little kitten, and told Ella she could have a goldfish instead. (Fluff was a little sad that Ella didn't have a goldfish, actually. *She* would have liked one.) But when she'd seen how upset Ella was, and understood that she really was old enough to look after a kitten properly, she'd changed her mind. Now she fussed over Fluff almost as much as Ella did. Fluff purred at the attention, and waved her paws idly. Ella's mum stroked the silky fur on Fluff's tummy, and laughed. She reached for the packet of cat treats on the counter. Fluff sprang out of her basket in half a second, standing on tiptoe with her paws against the cupboard door, scrabbling to get closer.

"I shouldn't be doing this." Mum shook her head. "You eat far too many of these. You'll get too big for your basket."

Fluff delicately nibbled the prawn-flavoured treat out of Mum's hand, and pranced back to her basket. She knew Ella's mum was joking. The basket was huge! Fluff liked to lie up against one edge of it, to make it seem a bit smaller. She had a feeling that Ella and her dad had gone a bit over the top in the pet shop.

After Fluff had run away from the farm to escape being taken home by a horrible boy who wanted to feed her to next door's German shepherd dog, Ella and her family had finally found her again a couple of days before Christmas. It had been the snowiest Christmas for twenty years, so Ella hadn't been able to go out and buy Fluff a Christmas present. She'd made up for it when the snow thawed, spending most of her Christmas money from Grandma on cat toys. Ella walked past a pet shop on her way home from school, and she liked to pop in and spend her pocket money on things for Fluff. Fluff didn't mind at all – she was *very* fond of those prawn-flavoured cat treats...

Suddenly, Fluff pricked up her ears. She could hear someone opening the front door. Ella was back from school!

"I'm home!" Ella called, and Fluff bounded up to the front door to twine herself round Ella's legs lovingly. She enjoyed having a nice sniff of the outdoors as well, poking her nose round the edge of the door.

Ella scooped her up gently. "Hey! No running off, Fluff!"

Fluff rubbed her head up and down Ella's chin. She wasn't trying to run off. It would just be fun to go and have a wander around outside. She hadn't been allowed out much since Ella and her family had adopted her, and sometimes it could be a little bit boring, being an indoor cat. Ella took her out in the garden at the weekends, but it was too dark when she got home from school. Fluff loved the garden, scratching the tree bark, chasing leaves, watching the bird table. She wished she could go and explore more when they were out, but she could see how worried Ella was about her getting lost again, so she stayed close by. Fluff thought it was a bit silly though – as if she could get lost by just investigating next door's garden! She'd only been lost before because she had been so young. She was a bit bigger now, and she could find her way anywhere, she was sure.

"I brought you home a present!" Ella said, as she shut the door. She carried Fluff into the kitchen, gave her mum a quick hug, and started to root around in her school bag.

"*Another* trip to the pet shop?" Mum asked, half-annoyed, half-laughing. "That cat is going to think it's Christmas every day."

Ella looked a little guilty. The pet shop was on her way home from school, and she was allowed to pop in, as long as she didn't take long. Mum liked to know where she was. "I know. But you did say she needed a collar. They haven't had any really nice ones before, but look at this!" She held up a beautiful blue leather collar. "Isn't it gorgeous? And look, it's got a place for her name and everything." She fastened it round Fluff's neck, and Fluff shook her head briskly, not sure about this new feeling.

"It's a bit big," Ella said, studying it thoughtfully. "But I suppose she'll grow into it, won't she? It looks beautiful." Dangling from the collar was a little round golden tag. "You could choose," Ella explained. "If I go back to the shop they can put her name on it. But I wanted to check what else we should put. Should we have our address engraved on it as well, in case she gets lost?"

Mum looked thoughtful for a moment. "Actually, I think just our phone number. Not even her name. I know it sounds silly, but if we put her name on, it means everyone knows it, and someone could call her over. We don't want anyone to find it easy to steal our gorgeous kitten, do we?"

Ella looked horrified. "No! I didn't think of that. Just the phone number then." She picked Fluff up again and held her tight, so tight that Fluff wriggled after a few seconds, trying to get down.

"Hey! Ella, it's OK. It's just a safety thing. It's really, really unlikely." Mum gave her an anxious look. "I know you love Fluff, and of course we don't want to lose her, but I think you're just worrying too much. Fluff's growing up now, and cats are very independent. I think you're going to have to let her out on her own soon."

Ella looked down at Fluff, who was now sniffing at the counter, hoping for more treats. "But what if she gets lost again?" she asked.

Mum sat down next to her. "There's no reason why she should, Ella. Cats have a really good sense of direction. She won't just go running off for no reason, she'll look around, make sure she knows how to get back. She's clever, isn't she?"

Ella nodded. "Yes," she agreed, and then she added doubtfully, "but she was lost before."

"She was really little then, and it wasn't her fault, anyway. She'd never been away from the farm. And she found you, didn't she? That shows you just how amazing her instincts are."

"Mmm." It was true. They'd never understood how Fluff had found her way back to them, but Ella couldn't believe it was just a coincidence.

"I think we ought to get Dad to put a cat flap in the back door. Then Fluff will be able to come in and out when she wants to."

"OK," Ella agreed reluctantly, still anxiously eyeing Fluff. She was such a small kitten, even now she'd grown a bit – and even with her podgy cat-treat-filled tummy. Would she really be safe out on her own?

At the weekend, Ella's dad went with her to the pet shop to buy Fluff a cat flap. It was the first time that Ella had been there and not enjoyed it. Normally she just wandered round wishing she had more money to buy presents for Fluff! Now she stared worriedly at the display of collars

while Dad and the pet shop owner discussed different sorts of cat flap. The engraved disk for Fluff's collar was ready for them to pick up, too, but Ella's excitement about it was almost gone. It had been replaced by a sense of relief that when Fluff went out of her new cat flap and disappeared, at least there was a chance that someone would find her and call.

The cat flap was a clever one that could be locked, or set so Fluff could only go through it one way. It was a pain to fit, though. Ella's dad had to saw a chunk out of the back door, and it took him ages. When it was finally finished, Ella crouched on the lawn waving the prawn-flavoured cat treats to tempt Fluff through. It didn't take her long to get the idea, although she looked very surprised when she first tried it. She had her front legs on the doorstep and her back legs in the kitchen, and she wasn't quite sure where her tummy was. She gave a panicked sort of wriggle, and suddenly all of her was in the garden. Fluff looked round suspiciously, not entirely sure how it had happened.

"Clever Fluff," Ella whispered, rewarding her with cat treats. "Do you like your new cat flap, mmm? You will be careful though, won't you?" She scratched Fluff's favourite behind-the-ears spot. "You stay close to the garden." Ella gulped. "No running out into the road, Fluff!"

Fluff purred as Ella petted her. She wasn't sure she completely understood this cat flap business yet, but it seemed to mean that she could just go out whenever she wanted to! And then get back in again for a snooze in her basket – it sounded brilliant to her, but she could hear in Ella's voice that she wasn't completely happy about it. She rubbed herself all round Ella twice in a comforting way, making her giggle. *I won't run away*, she promised. *Don't worry.*

For the first few days, Fluff kept her expeditions confined to the garden. There was plenty to explore there anyway. Ella had quite a big garden, long and narrow. Her mum loved gardening, and there were big flower beds, which Fluff wasn't much interested in, but also lots of exciting corners and pockets. Best of all was a tall old apple tree, its branches starting quite low to the ground. Ella had a swing in it, which she loved to sit and daydream on. The apple tree was Fluff's first real chance to practise climbing, and it made a brilliant claw-sharpener, too.

But after a little while, Fluff had found all the interesting things in her garden, and she scrambled up the fence to look down at next door. She'd seen Mrs Jones, Ella's neighbour, before. Ella had held Fluff up to the fence to be admired, and Mrs Jones had commented on her beautiful markings. Fluff hadn't had a chance to see much of the garden, but now she noticed something very exciting. She plunged down the other side of the fence with an undignified scrabble of claws, and stopped at the bottom for a calming lick of her ruffled fur. Then she set off to investigate. Mrs Jones's garden had a pond! With fish in it, Fluff soon discovered. She whiled away the rest of the afternoon perched on the rocks by the side of the water, dreamily watching the fish darting to and fro. Was it her imagination, or were they swimming slightly faster, looking a little more worried? Obviously she would need practice, but Fluff was fairly sure that if she dipped a paw in and held it still, she would be able to catch a fish…

Fluff was so interested in the fish that she almost forgot to get back to the house before Ella arrived home from school. She didn't want Ella to worry that she'd got lost, and of course, she loved to see her. She could always tell when it was nearly time for Ella to be back.

Fluff sprang up from her place on the rocks, and scooted halfway up Mrs Jones's fence before she'd even realized she was climbing. Then she nearly slid backwards, and had to jab her claws in hard to stay on. Embarrassed, she flung herself up and over and streaked across the lawn to the cat flap. Ella was just coming in the front door, and Mum laughed as Fluff shot through the flap.

"Just in time, Fluff! Oh, you're all out of breath."

Fluff glared up at her, and sat down in the middle of the kitchen floor, curling her tail round her legs in a dignified pose. She was trying not to look like a kitten who'd nearly fallen off a fence, but her whiskers were still twitchy with excitement. Outside might be a bit dangerous, but she did love it!

Chapter Two

It was mid-February, and it had suddenly got cold again. Ella was extra-glad to have Fluff sleeping on her feet at night. Mum and Dad had said that she was supposed to sleep in her basket, but they pretended not to notice that actually she always curled up with Ella. Mostly she stayed at the end of the bed, but a couple of times Ella had gone to sleep cuddling her, and Fluff slept snuggled under her chin.

Ella woke up early that morning. The duvet was huddled up around her shoulders where she'd wriggled herself down in the cold of the night. Fluff was pacing up and down the window sill, mewing excitedly.

"Fluff!" Ella moaned. "It's not even properly light yet, what's the matter?" Then she sat up, confused. It was almost light, but the room looked different somehow. And why was Fluff making such a fuss? Ella wrapped the duvet round her shoulders like a cloak and padded over to the window.

"Oh, wow! It's snowed again!" she exclaimed as she peered out.

It had snowed very heavily just before Christmas, when Fluff was lost, but the cold snap hadn't lasted long. January had just been grim and wet.

"Why does it have to be a school day?" Ella sighed. "It'll be too dark to play outside much after school."

Ella tried to argue at breakfast that school would probably be closed because of the snow, but Mum said it would have been announced on the radio. She promised faithfully to help Ella build an entire family of snowmen when she got back, and they dug out wellies and scarves and hats for the walk. Ella normally walked on her own to school. It wasn't very far, and she met up with lots of her friends, but today Mum said she'd go too, at least most of the way, because she was worried Ella might slip over in the snow.

"Don't go out today, Fluff," Ella said, as she struggled to pull her wellies on over two pairs of socks. "It's really cold, and the snow's very deep. You'd probably sink up to your whiskers. Stay in the house and keep nice and warm."

Fluff snuggled into her basket and snoozed for a while, but she was itching to go outside. Despite what Ella had said, Fluff really wanted to investigate the snow. She padded over to the cat flap and peered out. The snow was brand new and inviting. She couldn't see any tracks in it, just a sheet of crunchy, sparkling white. She pushed the cat flap open gently with her nose, and sniffed. The snow smelled so fresh, and she could hear the wind blowing through the trees, the snow falling from the branches with soft *whumpf* noises. How could she stay inside? She wouldn't go far…

Fluff eased herself out of the cat flap, shaking her paws daintily as they hit the snow. She knew all about snow, of course. Her long journey from the farm to Ella's house had nearly ended in disaster when she was caught in a snowstorm. But today she was just going for a quick look around. Nothing could go wrong. She'd explore the snowy garden, and as soon as she felt cold or tired, she could go back inside to warm up, and probably beg some cat treats from Ella's mum. Ella was just being too careful, Fluff thought. It was nice that Ella wanted to look after her, but really, she could look after herself!

Fluff's paws sank deeply into the snow. It must have been snowing for most of the night, as there was a thick layer over everything. The garden looked completely different, covered in strange lumps where the plants had been. Fluff looked down and saw her paw prints in the snow – the only ones. It was very exciting to be the only animal outside. She gave a little jump to make more prints, scattering her tracks around the lawn in a pattern.

It was still snowing a little, the flakes drifting down idly, tickling Fluff's whiskers. She sat up on her back legs and tried to catch them with her front paws, but the snowflakes floated on the wind, and it was hard to tell where they were going. One particularly large flake came twirling down past Fluff's nose, and she whisked her paws at it. It seemed to dodge, she twirled around to chase it and suddenly she was flat on her tummy in the snow. Fluff stood up quickly, checking that no one had seen her slide. The snowflake had disappeared into the thousands of other snowflakes, and Fluff spat snow out of her mouth crossly. She plunged off across the garden to find something else to do.

Suddenly she noticed that hers weren't the only tracks any more. A delicate pattern of forked prints was spattered over the snow by the fence. And perched on top of the fence, eyeing her cautiously, was a blackbird!

It whistled shrilly and hopped down into the next-door garden. Fluff trotted along the path of tracks eagerly. She'd got the hang of walking in the snow again now, lifting her paws higher than usual. The tracks led underneath the fence, and Fluff wriggled after them, not even remembering that she'd planned to stay in her own garden. The blackbird was on the bird table now, gobbling breadcrumbs that she'd put out. It must have been that morning, because Fluff could see the prints of Mrs Jones's wellies in the snow. She gazed hopefully up at the blackbird for a while, but it just squawked and chattered at her angrily. Clearly it didn't fancy coming down to be chased.

She hopped from footprint to footprint instead, and realized that Mrs Jones must have gone down to check on the pond as well. Her prints led right up to the edge. Fluff stood in them and leaned over to look. The pond was frozen! She could see the water-plants poking out in places, snow drifted up around them, but most of the pond was covered with strange, clear, greenish ice. Fluff couldn't see the fish at all, they must be hiding away at the bottom. Cautiously, she put a paw on the ice, and it skidded. She jumped back quickly. She'd already fallen over once, and the ice was horribly cold.

The pond was close to Mrs Jones's fence, and there was an inviting gap underneath. The next garden smelled really interesting; somehow the cold was making all the smells so much better! Fluff flattened herself to the ground and squirmed through the gap, her whiskers twitching excitedly. Then she squirmed some more, and then she wriggled. Then she stopped wriggling. She wasn't going anywhere. She was stuck!

Chapter Three

Fluff hunched her shoulders worriedly, trying to work out what had gone wrong. The gap had looked perfectly big enough – her whiskers had fitted through, so the rest of her should have been able to. Then she realized – it was her collar. It had caught on something, maybe a nail sticking out of the fence. Suddenly Fluff panicked and started to struggle, pulling backwards and forwards desperately, mewing frantically and scrabbling with her paws. She mewed for Ella to come and help her, forgetting that Ella was at school. But after a couple of minutes she was too exhausted to struggle any longer, and she slumped to the ground, her neck aching where the collar was pulling at her.

Fluff lay panting miserably, wondering what to do. She supposed she would just have to wait for someone to rescue her. When she didn't get home in time to meet Ella from school, they would start to worry, wouldn't they? Or maybe Mrs Jones would come out to look at her pond again. Fluff shivered. It was going to be a horribly long, cold wait.

Fluff mewed with frustration. It was just so stupid. Her collar was too big, and it had got caught. It wasn't her fault! She gave a furious wriggle, and suddenly felt the collar stretch. Perhaps instead of trying to pull the collar off the fence, she should be trying to get out of the collar altogether. She pulled downwards, trying to stretch the collar even more. It hurt a bit, but the collar did seem to give. Now if she could just pull herself backwards…

Fluff popped out of the collar, feeling as though she might have pulled her ears off. She twitched them. No, they were still there. She'd done it! Feeling very proud of herself, she examined the collar. There wasn't a nail, just a sharp splinter of wood sticking out of the fence. Fluff hadn't been as far as the next garden on her travels before, so as she came out from under the fence she looked around carefully, trying to work out if this was another cat's territory, or even worse, if there was a dog around. Everything smelled all right, but she wasn't sure how the snow changed smells, and she wanted to be extra cautious. As she sat watching, she noticed a strange metal thing in the middle of the garden, a pole, with things hanging from it. Fluff sat with her head on one side, trying to work out what it might be. Suddenly two birds flew down to perch on the hanging bits, and she realized it was full of birdseed. Fluff's ears pricked forward, and she sank into a hunting crouch. If only she could get closer… Fluff hadn't had much opportunity to practise her hunting skills yet, but she was keen to learn. Her mother had tried to teach her how to catch mice back at the farm, but Fluff thought birds looked more fun to chase.

With a heavy flumping sound, a pair of enormously fat wood pigeons thumped down on to the snowy grass. They were too big to perch on the feeders, but there were a few bits of seed and nuts scattered about in the snow underneath, and the pigeons set to gobbling them up greedily.

Fluff's heart began to beat faster with excitement. This was her chance! How pleased Ella would be if Fluff brought her back a pigeon! She left her hiding place and crawled closer on her tummy, low to the ground, her paws muffled by the snow. The pigeons completely ignored her, too busy making sure they didn't miss any bits of seed that might be half-buried in the snow. With a massive burst of energy, Fluff pounced, fastening her teeth into the tail of the nearest pigeon, which let out a loud squawk of surprise. She'd done it! She'd actually caught something!

The pigeon looked round, saw that it was being attacked by a cat in the middle of its lunch, and panicked. All right, so it was only a very small cat, but then pigeons are known for having very small brains.

Squawking in horror, the pigeon tried to fly away, but this was a bit difficult with a cat attached to a vital part of its flying equipment. Fluff hung on grimly as the wings beat up and down. Her first catch was *not* getting away. Seeing that flapping wasn't going to work, the pigeon changed its tactics, and began to run *and* flap, trying to build up some speed to help lift itself off the ground. Rather like a feathery plane thundering down the runway, it set off across the lawn. Fluff was dragged along behind like a waterskier, her paws making great tracks in the snow.

At last the pigeon managed enough lift and pulled itself off the ground with a mighty effort, taking Fluff with it. Her front paws left the ground, and she peered down worriedly. Surely the pigeon couldn't actually fly off with her… There was no way she was going to let go! Luckily for Fluff, the tail gave up instead. A great clump of feathers came right out, and the pigeon flew off looking decidedly bald. It landed clumsily at the top of a nearby tree, and squawked abuse at Fluff, furiously preening its mangled tail. Fluff sat on the ground, panting and spitting feathers. Did that count as catching a pigeon? she wondered. Could she claim it as half a pigeon, perhaps? She heaved a happy sigh, and spat out a last feather.

Fluff gazed up at the pigeon, still angrily squawking at her, and noticed that it had started to snow again. She danced around the lawn, pouncing on the twirling snowflakes. This was so much fun! It was cold, of course, but her thick fur was keeping her cosy, and in a few minutes she would head back to her cat flap and the lovely warm house. She chased round and round, whisking her tail, still full of excitement after her hunt. The snow was coming in big, thick flakes now, large enough to snap at with her teeth.

Fluff was enjoying herself so much that she didn't notice how heavy the snow was becoming. The pigeons and the other birds had disappeared, and it was terribly quiet. Fluff opened her mouth and tried to catch a particularly plump and dizzy snowflake, and then looked around in surprise. She couldn't see! The whole garden was a mass of whirling white and grey, and Fluff couldn't see anything beyond two whisker-lengths away. She shuddered. This was too much like her scary journey a couple of months before. She needed to get home at once. But – where was home? Fluff gulped. She couldn't even see the fence.

A gust of icy wind rushed at Fluff, and she felt as though it had blown right through her. Her ears were laid back against her head, and the snowflakes felt like stabbing needles as they blew into her fur.

Worriedly, she peered around her. She could just about see the tree that the pigeon had flown into, so the fence must be over there somewhere. Leaning into the wind, she ploughed forward. It was so cold now! Oh, at last, there was the fence. Fluff's panicky feeling eased a little. She only had to get across next-door's garden and she would be home. She wriggled under the fence, and then followed her nose straight across. She was nearly there – and once she was back home, she was *not* coming out again. Not till it stopped snowing, anyway.

Fluff almost bumped into the next fence, but she didn't mind, she was just so glad to see it. She popped out from underneath; she was back in her garden!

Except – this didn't look like her garden. Even with the snow everywhere, it didn't feel right. Ella's garden had lots of little walls and hedges and things, but this garden was big and flat. Had she miscounted the number of fences? Fluff didn't think she'd gone into another garden after next-door-but-one, but perhaps in the excitement of exploring, she had…?

Feeling frightened, she scurried across this strange garden to the next fence, hoping desperately that this time she would see somewhere she knew. The snow was drifting up against the fences now, and she had to half-burrow through. Hopefully, she pushed the snow out of the way with her nose, and stared around. This garden was full of play equipment, a slide and a little wooden house, half covered in snow. Fluff had never been here before.

Fluff had gone the wrong way in the storm – and now she was completely lost!

Chapter Four

Fluff stood still for a while, sniffing the air, hoping to catch a familiar scent that would lead her home. But the snow deadened the smells as well as the noises, and Fluff felt completely blind. What should she do? Had she gone past Ella's house in the storm somehow? Should she be going back or forwards?

One thing was certain. She *had* to move somewhere. Sitting still wouldn't keep her warm. She could feel the cold seeping into her bones – even her whiskers ached with it. The awful thing was, she might be going even further away from home! Miserably, Fluff forced her paws to keep plodding on through the deep snow. Without realizing, she slipped through a gap in a broken-down old fence at the bottom of a garden, and strayed into the old wood that ran along behind the houses on Ella's street. It was even harder going. She was wading through drifted snow under tall and menacing trees. Fluff knew she'd never been anywhere like this before, and it made her shudder. The trees seemed to wave their dark arms at her, and their roots tripped her up. It felt as though they did it on purpose, sending her rolling into hollows of deep snow, so she had to struggle and fight her way out. Every time it happened, Fluff grew just a little bit more tired.

It was getting dark, and even harder to see. Fluff wished sadly that she had listened to Ella, and never gone out in the snow. She still didn't quite understand how she had managed to get so lost. One minute she had known exactly where she was, and the next she'd had no idea. It had all happened so fast. Fluff shivered. There was nothing she could do about it now. She needed to rest, but where could she go? There were a few places under the trees, where the roots had made little burrows, but they didn't look very warm. Fluff needed somewhere out of the biting wind.

Suddenly, something loomed up out of the gloom. Fluff peered forward doubtfully. It certainly wasn't a tree. In fact, it looked more like a house.

With a fresh burst of energy, she trotted forward, picking her way carefully over the snow. It was a tumbledown old cottage, built for the gamekeeper who guarded the wood, but it had been empty now for years and years. The door was boarded up, but there were plenty of holes where a small cat could creep in. Fluff sighed with relief as she squeezed herself between the boards. Even just inside the door the difference was wonderful – no more freezing wind slicing through her fur.

Staggering with tiredness, Fluff headed further in, looking for somewhere comfortable to sleep. Gratefully she spotted a pile of old blankets in one corner. They were smelly and stained, but Fluff wasn't feeling fussy. She burrowed in, wanting to be as warm as possible, and hollowed herself out a little nest in the rags. She closed her eyes, wrapped her tail round her nose, and let a warm tide of sleep wash over her. All at once she was back home, with Ella, being stroked, and fed cat treats.

But then she heard a noise. Fluff twitched in her sleep, fighting to stay in her lovely dream. Oh, she didn't *want* to wake up, and be back in this cold, real adventure! Something was breaking into her dream – a mewing sound. Fluff sighed. It was no good, she wasn't asleep any more. She poked her head up from her blanket nest, and gazed round grumpily. She couldn't see anything, and the cottage was silent, except for the eerie shrieking of the wind outside. Was it that she'd heard? It must have been. Fluff was just settling back down to sleep when she heard the mewing again.

Something was crying for help!

Ella rushed home – as fast as she could in slippery wellies – full of news about her fun day. School had been all about snow – talking about snowflake patterns in science, writing snow poems in English, and lots and lots of playing outside in the snow at lunch and break.

"We had a brilliant snowball fight," Ella told her mum happily, as she watched her make a mug of hot chocolate. "Oooh, can I have marshmallows, please? Excellent." She took the chocolate and sat down, sipping it slowly. "Yum. It's so cold out there, Mum, my fingers are freezing, even though I had my gloves on." She gripped the warm mug tightly. "They're only just thawing out." Ella took a big mouthful of chocolate, and sighed happily. It was nice to be back inside. "It's so cool that it's Friday, and we've got the whole weekend free. Can we go sledging in the park tomorrow?" Then she looked round, suddenly realizing that she hadn't seen Fluff since she got back. "Mum, where's Fluff? She didn't go out, did she?" Ella asked anxiously.

Her mum looked surprised. "But she's got her cat flap now, Ella, she's allowed outside! I saw her playing in the garden earlier."

Ella looked worried. "I told her not to. I was scared she'd get lost in the snow again. I suppose it was silly to think she wouldn't go out."

"I don't think you need to worry, Ella," her mum said reassuringly. "Fluff's not a baby any more. I know she's still tiny, but she *has* grown! She's definitely old enough to be out there."

"But it's been snowing really hard today, Mum! And Fluff *always* comes back to see me when I get home from school. Always." Ella got up to peer out of the kitchen window. "The snow's really deep in the garden. She could easily have got confused about where she was going. Oh, why didn't I just lock the cat flap?"

"Ella, it's not fair to lock it, unless we really need to. Fluff wouldn't understand why she couldn't go out. She'd just get upset." But Ella's mum came to join her at the window. "You're right though, it *is* odd that she isn't back yet. I wonder where she's got to."

"We should go out and look for her," Ella said, heading for the hallway to put all her outdoor things back on.

"Oh, Ella, no, I'm sure we don't need to. Sit down, finish your hot chocolate. Honestly, Fluff was having a lovely time out there earlier on. She was playing with the snowflakes. She's probably just got too caught up with exploring. I'm sure she'll be home in a minute."

Ella trailed reluctantly back to the table. She knew Mum was right, but something was still niggling at her. Fluff had *never* missed meeting her before.

Ella's mum didn't sit back down, but stayed thoughtfully staring out of the window. She wished she was as sure as she was making out to Ella. She didn't think Fluff was lost, but she *was* worried. Fluff should have been back – was she hiding out somewhere, waiting for the snow to stop? She just couldn't help feeling that it was an awfully cold day for a small kitten to be stuck outside...

Fluff stood up, her whiskers twitching. Usually hearing another cat would have made her fur stand on end, and she'd be wanting to fight and defend her territory. But there was something about that cry. She didn't think that the cat making that noise was going to be putting up much of a fight. She picked her way out of her blanket nest, and stood still, listening carefully. She'd been so sleepy when she heard the mewing that she wasn't quite sure where it had come from.

There it was again. So quiet. So weak. Fluff listened anxiously. The other cat wasn't in this room, she was almost sure. She picked her way over the rubbish and fallen bricks, and peered through the doorway.

The cottage was tiny, only two rooms. The inner room was full of broken furniture, and Fluff leaped up on to an old chair to try and see what was happening. The room was silent, and she looked around worriedly. She was sure she hadn't imagined it. Although – the mew had seemed to be part of her dream at first... No! There it was again. The cry was coming from a battered cupboard on the other side of the room. Fluff wove her way carefully through the junk, and nosed at the door.

It swung open slightly, and cautiously she stuck her head inside.

Staring back at her out of the gloom was an enormous pair of green eyes.

The mew came again, and Fluff watched in horror as a tiny white kitten struggled to its feet, desperately trying to reach her.

The kitten could hardly stand, and at once Fluff jumped into the cupboard, nosing the little creature gently. She towered over it. This kitten was far too young to be on her own! She looked as though she was only just old enough to eat food, rather than milk from her mother. Where *was* her mother? Fluff could smell that at least one other cat had been here. Maybe this was where the kitten had been born. Cats often chose odd places to have their kittens – *she* had been born in a stable, and the horse it belonged to hadn't been happy at all.

But the mother cat's scent was fading. This kitten had been alone for a while, Fluff thought. She had to be starving. She was nuzzling hopefully at

Fluff, as though she thought Fluff might have brought her some food, but eventually she gave up, and collapsed down again. The cupboard was lined with rags, like the nest Fluff had made, and the white kitten lay down, curling herself up tight. She looked cold. Fluff lay down gently, curling herself around the kitten, like her own mother used to snuggle up to Fluff and her brothers and sisters.

The kitten mewed again, an even smaller sound this time, but she sounded pleased. Fluff purred comfortingly. *Go to sleep. Maybe we can find your mother,* she thought. But she had a horrible feeling that the kitten's mother was far away. Somehow they'd been separated.

Fluff rested her head gently next to the little white ears, watching anxiously as the kitten twitched her way to sleep. Fluff's tummy rumbled, but at least she'd had breakfast, which was more than she guessed the kitten had. She could feel the tiny body warming up, and her own eyes began to close.

Curled around each other, the two cats slept, alone in the snowy night.

Chapter Five

Ella got up at six the next morning. It was still practically dark, but she didn't care. She felt as though she hadn't slept at all, though she supposed she must have done. All her plans for a weekend of fun in the snow had gone – Fluff still wasn't back. Ella went downstairs, put on her winter coat, hat and scarf, and unlocked the back door.

The cat flap swung open as she went out, and she felt like kicking it. She *should* have locked it, no matter what Mum said. She would rather have a grumpy Fluff than no Fluff at all.

Out in the back garden the snow looked even deeper. There must have been another big fall in the night. Ella shivered. It was really freezing, even wrapped up as she was. She sighed. The garden looked so beautiful, all white with patches of green and icicles hanging from the branches. It was like a Christmas card – there was even a robin perched on the fence, looking at her hopefully to see if she was about to put crumbs out. Ella smiled a very small smile. If Fluff had been here, she would have been jumping up and down under the fence trying to get him. But all that proved was that Fluff definitely *wasn't* anywhere in the garden. Tucking her hands under her arms to try and keep them warm, Ella walked down the path – or rather, where she thought the path ought to be, as she couldn't see it at all.

"Fluff! Fluff, come on. Breakfast!" she called, trying to sound cheerful.

She stared round the garden, willing a stripy little furry body to come shooting out of the bushes. Then her heart leaped as she saw something moving at the bottom of the garden. "Fluff!" she squeaked delightedly, running towards her. "Oh, Fluff, you had me so worried. You bad cat, I thought I'd lost you again. Oh!" Ella stopped still as the strange cat stared up at her in surprise. It looked rather offended – as though it had been minding its own business, going for a morning walk, and suddenly it was being chased by a screaming girl. It twitched its tail irritably, and strolled on over the snow in a very dignified and haughty way, deliberately ignoring Ella.

"Sorry..." Ella whispered after it. She knew it was stupid to apologize to a cat, but it seemed to be the kind of cat who would expect her to. Now she could see it properly, it didn't even look much like Fluff. It was loads bigger, and its tabby coat was more spotted than striped. Trying not to cry, she plodded back to the house.

Her parents were in the kitchen making breakfast. They were both dressed, which wasn't normal for a Saturday. Usually everyone got up slowly, enjoying the weekend.

"Any luck?" Ella's dad asked. "We heard you calling."

Ella shook her head.

"I thought I saw her," she said miserably. "But it was another cat."

"I'm sure she's just waiting for the snow to stop," Ella's mum said briskly. "She'll be back soon. Sit down and have some breakfast, Ella."

"The snow *has* stopped," Ella pointed out, as she perched on the very edge of a chair. "So why isn't she back?"

Ella's parents glanced at each other with raised eyebrows, and she glared at them. "You're not taking this seriously!" she burst out. "Fluff's lost, I'm sure she is. We have to go and look for her."

Her dad sighed. "I have to say, I'm surprised she isn't back. She's never stayed out this long before, has she?"

Ella's mum nodded reluctantly. "I suppose not. I've just been hoping she'd pop through the cat flap any minute, but maybe we should go and look for her.

We should probably start by asking the neighbours if they've seen her."

Ella leaped up from the chair, heading for the door.

"Ella!" her mum yelled after her. "It's half-past six! On a Saturday! You cannot go and wake up the whole street. Eat some breakfast first."

A couple of hours later, Ella and her parents had asked up and down the street, but no one had seen Fluff. Everyone was upset to hear she was missing – lots of the neighbours had said how sweet she was, and how she often came up to be stroked and fussed over. Ella's parents had asked people to keep an eye out, and check that she wasn't shut in any garages or sheds.

"Mrs Jones's curtains are open now," Ella pointed out, as they trudged back up the street. "Can we go and ask her? Fluff loves her garden, she spends ages watching her fish in the pond."

"We might as well," her mum agreed.

Mrs Jones was horrified. "Poor thing," she said, sounding really worried. "It's so cold out. Oh, Ella, I'm sorry," she added, seeing Ella's eyes fill with tears. "You must be beside yourself, especially with her being lost before. I'm sure she'll turn up. She's such a bright little thing. She's probably just found herself a nice warm spot to see the snow out."

"Have you been out in your garden?" Ella said, sniffing. "She might be by your pond."

"The pond's frozen," Mrs Jones replied. "I saw her looking at it yesterday, she seemed very confused." She shook her head. "I don't think she's out there now, Ella, but you're welcome to go and check." She held the door open. "Why don't you all come and have a cup of tea, you must be freezing."

She led the way into the kitchen, and unlocked her garden door for Ella to go out. Ella's parents sat down gratefully. They were just sipping the tea, when Ella dashed back in, tears streaming down her face.

"Ella! What is it?" her mum asked, leaping up. "What's happened? Is Fluff—?"

Gulping, Ella stretched out her hand, and laid something small and wet on the table next to the teacups.

It was Fluff's collar.

Fluff woke up as a cold draught cut through the door to the cupboard, and made her flicker her ears uneasily. It took a few moments for her to work out where she was, then she looked down worriedly at the white kitten. She was curled into a tiny ball, right up against Fluff's tummy, and she was deeply asleep. Fluff licked her gently, and she laid her ears back, but didn't wake up. Fluff knew that she had to try and find her way home. Ella would be desperate, and the longer she left it, the harder it would be to find any tracks to help her get back. And she was starving! She'd missed her tea, and breakfast. That made her feel guilty, though – who knew when the younger kitten had last had anything to eat? Fluff eyed her thoughtfully. She hadn't sounded hungry last night. Was she so weak that she'd forgotten to be hungry? That was bad, very bad. Fluff needed to get home at once, and the little one had to wake up and come too. Fluff nosed her firmly, and she gave a faint, complaining mew, then opened her green eyes and stared accusingly at Fluff.

Fluff licked her again, apologetically, then butted her in the chest to make her stand up. The kitten mewed miserably, and tottered to her feet. Fluff stared at her, suddenly realizing that even now she was warmed up, this tiny creature was not going anywhere.

Fluff had found it almost impossible to stagger through the snow the day before – and this kitten was very weak!

But what should Fluff do? She didn't want to leave the kitten behind, either. Helplessly, she watched as the little white cat gave another feeble mew and slumped back down again. No, she certainly wasn't coming on an expedition through the snow. Fluff would just have to go and find Ella, and bring her back to help. The wailing wind had died down now, leaving an eerie silence, and Fluff thought the snow must have stopped. She would be able to see where she was heading. She felt better now she had made a decision, and she nosed her way out of the cupboard, and across the room.

She wanted to find some of the rags of blanket she had curled up in yesterday. The kitten wasn't so frozen now, but without Fluff to keep her warm, she would quickly get cold again. Dragging the blanket back with her teeth, she wrapped it round the kitten.

A tiny purr rumbled through the scrap of white fur, making Fluff feel even more determined. She had to find help. Giving the kitten one last worried glance, she pushed the cupboard door to with her nose to keep the cold out, and set off.

Fluff peered cautiously out of the hole in the cottage door, and shivered. The snow was even deeper now, but at least it seemed to have frozen hard. She stepped out, and looked helplessly around. Which way should she go? She had no idea. Even if she'd been able to remember which way she'd come, it all looked different now. Even the smells were covered in snow. She took a few uncertain steps, hoping to recognize something soon.

Then, to her horror, Fluff noticed snowflakes spiralling down. More snow! She looked up, hoping it would be just a light shower, but the sky was full of them, falling thickly down towards her. She needed to get back under cover fast – she knew from yesterday that there was no point trying to go anywhere in this. But perhaps she had time to find some food, before the storm got too heavy? Fluff looked around hopefully, but only saw trees. No good.

Hurrying back into the cottage, she noticed something she'd not seen in the dark the evening before. A battered old bag, lying by the door. Eagerly, Fluff clawed at it, retrieving a foil-wrapped packet. Ham sandwiches!

They didn't smell very fresh, but she was in no position to be fussy, and neither was the kitten.

The kitten did *not* want to be woken again. Fluff had to cuff her nose to make her sit up and take notice of the food. She sniffed at it reluctantly, too tired to bother, but Fluff knew the kitten had to eat. She bit off a tiny piece of ham, and then nudged it against the kitten's mouth until she opened it to protest. As the taste of the food hit her tongue, she brightened a little, swallowing it down, and looked hopefully at Fluff for more. Fluff bit off some more pieces, gulping a few down herself. The kitten managed several mouthfuls, then curled up to sleep again.

Fluff watched her, feeling relieved. Surely the food would help her? She devoured the rest of the sandwich, then tucked herself back round the kitten. There didn't seem to be much else to do but sleep, so she slept.

It was much, much colder when she woke again. She was shivering, even wrapped up in their blanket nest. The kitten wasn't. She was completely still, and for an awful moment Fluff thought she wasn't even breathing.

There was a tiny snuffle of breath, but it was so shallow – as though the kitten could hardly be bothered. When Fluff tried to rouse her, she wouldn't wake. She was too cold.

Fluff stood up. The cold seemed to be inside her now, a freezing fear that she wouldn't be able to save this little one. The kitten had no one to help her but Fluff. Even if it was still snowing, she had go, *now*, and find Ella, and bring her back.

Chapter Six

Fluff staggered through the snow, her paws aching with the cold. Every so often she had to stop and rest, taking in deep shaking breaths of the burning cold air, and each time it was harder to set off again. But she couldn't give up. She was desperate to find Ella now. If Fluff could just keep going, surely she would find her soon, and she'd be home and in the warm, and Ella would be able to help the snow-white kitten. She ploughed on, trying not to think of the cold, just imagining the big bowl of tuna fish that Ella would give her…

"Ella, sweetheart, we have to go back home now. It's turned really cold – it's not good for us to be out in this for so long." Ella's mum was looking really anxious.

"But Mum, Fluff's out in it!" Ella cried. "And she's tiny and she isn't wearing a great big coat and boots and a hat and—"

"Yes, yes, I know." Mum sighed. "Just a little longer then. We've been up and down the street twice now though, I don't know where else to look."

"What about that little wood that backs on to the gardens further down?" Ella's dad suggested.

"Well, yes, I suppose she could have got in there," Mum agreed doubtfully. "It's worth a try."

"There's an alleyway round the corner, we can get in that way." Dad strode off, Ella trotting beside him.

They were a few steps in among the trees when Mum held Ella back. "I'm not sure this is a good idea after all," she told Ella. "The snow must have blown right in here, it's really deep, and there's bound to be tree roots and things hidden under the snowdrifts. You could break an ankle."

"Mmmm." Ella's dad looked thoughtful. "You're right. Maybe we should poke a branch into the snow to make sure we aren't about to fall into anything dangerous."

Ella wasn't listening. Letting go of her dad's arm, she took a shaky step forward, and crouched down. Her parents watched in amazement as a tiny grey shape staggered towards them through the gloomy, snow-filled wood. Ella was crying, tears tracking down her face without her even noticing.

Fluff put on a burst of speed and shot into Ella's arms, curling her head joyfully in under Ella's chin, and purring with relief and happiness. She'd found Ella. She was back. She was safe.

For a few moments she allowed herself to enjoy being stroked and cuddled and told how brave she was, and how naughty to go running off in the snow. Then she wriggled herself out from Ella's tight embrace, putting her paws against Ella's chest and mewing urgently.

"What's the matter?" Ella looked confused. Fluff had seemed so happy to see them, but now it was obvious that she wanted something.

Fluff struggled out of Ella's arms and jumped lightly down, looking back up at Ella, and mewing again. *Follow me!* she was saying, as clearly as she could. She trotted a few paces back into the wood, and looked round at Ella beseechingly.

“What’s she doing?” Dad asked. “Fluff, that’s not the way home. Come on!”

“She wants us to follow her,” Ella said firmly. “Look, she’s calling us.” And she set off after Fluff, who bounded ahead delightedly, all her tiredness gone. Only a few moments before, she had felt as though she was going to drop down in the snow and sleep. She had been struggling through the drifts for over an hour, trying to find any signs of the way home. But now she was back with Ella, she had a surge of new energy.

"Ella, be careful!" her mum called. "Don't trip over any fallen branches!" Ella's parents scrambled after them. They had no idea where they were going, but it was clear that Fluff was trying to get them to follow, anyone could see that. Every so often she would turn round to check they were still with her, then head off again, following her paw prints purposefully back through the trees.

There it was! Fluff jumped through the door of the cottage, popping her head back out to call to Ella. Ella crouched down to squeeze through the gap in the door after her.

"Ella, no!" her mum yelled. "Be careful, you don't know what's in there!"

"It's OK, Mum," Ella called back. "I'm following Fluff, it's fine."

Her mother tried to catch her up and stop her, worried that the old building might be falling down, but she slipped on the snow, and slid over, falling on to her hands and knees just in time to see Ella disappearing into the building. Ella's dad stopped to help her up, and they skidded over to look through the window.

Fluff wove her way hurriedly through the cottage, still calling to Ella to follow.

"I'm coming, I'm coming, Fluff! I can't fit underneath all this stuff like you can!" Ella puffed, scrambling over a pile of old sofa cushions. "I wish I knew what you were trying to show me, anyway." She realized that Fluff had stopped next to an old cupboard that was jammed up against the far wall. She was peering round the door, her body tense, nervous, almost scared – as though she wasn't sure what she was going to find. Ella walked quietly up to Fluff, and knelt behind her, but she couldn't see what Fluff was looking at. Suddenly some of the stiffness went out of Fluff's spine, and she reached gently into the cupboard. She backed carefully out, carrying something in her mouth – something quite large. She dropped it in Ella's lap, and it was only as Fluff sat back and gazed hopefully up at her, that Ella realized what it was. Fluff had just given her a kitten! She had pulled it out of the cupboard like a magic trick.

"Fluff! It's a kitten! Where did you—?"

Fluff mewed urgently at her, and Ella looked more closely. She stroked the tiny white head, and saw that the little creature didn't stir. She gave Fluff an anxious look, her heart thudding with nervousness. Fluff looked back up at her lovingly.

"I don't know," Ella said worriedly. "She's so little and weak, Fluff. I – I'm not even sure she's still breathing." She stood up, cradling the tiny furry ball gently. "Come on. We need to get her to a vet." Very carefully she wrapped the kitten in her scarf, and tucked the parcel inside her jacket. She wasn't sure she could clamber over all that junk carrying her.

Ella's parents were calling her as they headed back, and her dad was starting to pull away the boards blocking the door.

"Ella! There you are!" he said angrily as she crouched to go through the hole. "What have you been doing? You should never have gone in there; what have we told you about playing in dangerous places like that?"

"I wasn't playing, Dad!" Ella said indignantly. "Look!" And she opened her jacket to show them her tiny passenger. "Fluff found her. But I'm not sure—" Her voice wobbled. "I can't see her breathing," she whispered, tears stinging the corners of her eyes.

"Let me see." Her dad lifted the kitten out, and she lay floppy and lifeless in his big hands. He was silent for a horribly long moment. "She is. But only just. Come on, we need to get home right now and ring the vet. We need to tell them we've got an emergency coming in."

Ella had been to the vet's surgery before, to take Fluff to have all her vaccinations, but this time there was no hanging around in the reception. She and her parents raced in, Ella cradling the kitten, and were rushed straight through to the surgery. It was the same vet who'd looked after Fluff before, and she smiled, recognizing Ella.

"The receptionist said you'd found a stray kitten?" she asked, gently taking the scarf-wrapped bundle from Ella.

Ella nodded. "She's so tiny, and she's only just breathing," she explained. "It wasn't really us that found her though, it was Fluff."

"We think she must have been

abandoned by her mother," Ella's dad put in. "Fluff and Ella found her in an old cottage on some woodland near us."

The vet nodded thoughtfully. "She looks about three or four weeks old to me. Only just old enough to survive without her mother. She's very weak – I think she's had a couple of days on her own in the cold. I'm going to put her on a drip to get some food into her, and we'll put her in an incubator, get her really nice and warm." She smiled, looking at Ella's anxious face. "I think you found her just in time. I can't promise, but it looks to me as if she's just cold and hungry, nothing worse. You might even be able to take her home in a couple of hours." She started to get the equipment she needed.

"Oh, that's fantastic!" Ella squeaked, not noticing that Mum and Dad looked a bit shocked. "That's really good, because I don't think Fluff will understand where she is. She looked so upset when we drove off. She was watching us through the window—"

"Ella, Ella, hang on," Mum interrupted. "We don't know who this kitten belongs to. And we already have Fluff, I'm not sure we can—"

"Mum!" Ella was horrified. "We have to take her home! Fluff saved her – what are you going to tell Fluff if we go back without her?"

Dad looked thoughtful. "Didn't the people who moved from that house down the road a few days ago have a white cat? I'm sure I remember seeing one around. Was she pregnant? Maybe she decided to have her kittens in that cottage. Cats do that sometimes, don't they?" he asked the vet. "Find strange places to have their kittens?"

The vet nodded. "It's to do with wanting to be private, and keeping the kittens safe. If her owners were moving, she might not have liked all the mess of packing up at home." She was laying the white kitten in what looked like a fish tank. "This has got a heat mat to warm her up gently," she explained. "I'll take her through to the ward when she's settled."

Ella peered through the plastic side. The kitten looked really cosy, but that gave her a horrible thought. "What happened to the other kittens?" she asked worriedly. "Do you think they're outside somewhere? There was only this little one in the cupboard."

"Maybe the mother carried them back to the house," the vet said thoughtfully. "Or perhaps she only had the one. That happens sometimes, and it would mean that it wasn't too obvious she was going to have kittens. Her owners might not have known."

Mum looked sad. "So they took her with them and left the kitten behind."

"Yes, she might have had to go home for some food. Thank goodness for Fluff," the vet said, smiling.

Mum sighed, and shook her head. "I suppose you're right, Ella. After what Fluff did, we have to take this one home too." Then she smiled. "I might have known it wouldn't stop with one!"

"You mean we can keep her?" Ella asked, hopping up and down. "Really?"

Her dad grinned. "Why not. I took ages putting in that cat flap, we might as well use it... Ooof!" he gasped as Ella hurled herself at him for a hug.

"Thank you, thank you, thank you! I can't wait to tell Fluff!"

Back at home Fluff was sitting anxiously on the window sill. She didn't quite understand where Ella and the kitten had gone, but Ella had whispered that they were looking after her. She stared out at the snowy street, watching for the car, waiting for Ella. As they pulled up in front of the house, she jumped up with her paws scrabbling on the glass, mewing excitedly. Where was the kitten?

Ella got carefully out of the car, and Fluff watched in relief as she walked slowly up the path, cradling the kitten. Fluff was there waiting as they opened the door, twining affectionately around Ella's ankles, then leading Ella to the kitchen and her too-big basket. She watched as Ella carefully set the kitten down on the red cushion, then she stepped in and curled herself around the white kitten lovingly. The kitten, who'd been fast asleep ever since they left the vet's, opened one eye sleepily, and looked up at Fluff. "Prrrp," she murmured, and a very small bright-pink tongue shot out and licked Fluff's nose. Then she went back to sleep.

Fluff looked down at her, and then back at Ella, who was crouched next to the basket watching.

Ella reached over to scratch Fluff under the chin. "What shall we call her?" she wondered, looking at the kitten's white fur, snuggled next to Fluff's tabby coat. "How about Snowy?

She *is* our snow rescue kitten."

Fluff yawned and stretched a little in agreement.

Ella grinned, watching the two of them snooze. "It looks like we were right to buy a big basket after all!"

The Curious Kitten

For George

Chapter One

Amber rolled the jingly cat ball down the length of the hallway and giggled as Cleo flung herself after it, her paws slipping on the wooden floor. She loved the way the kitten took chasing the ball so seriously!

Her mum opened the kitchen door and gasped as she almost tripped over the skidding kitten. "Oh, Cleo!

I nearly kicked you. Are you all right?"

But Cleo didn't even seem to have noticed. She had finally caught her jingly ball and was rolling over and over with it, growling fierce kitten growls.

"I don't think that ball's coming out alive," Mum commented, smiling. "Amber, did you finish sorting out all your new pencils and things for school? Have you packed them in your rucksack?"

Amber nodded. "Everything's ready." She got up, looking worriedly between Mum and Cleo. "Mum, what's going to happen to Cleo while

I'm at school?"

"What do you mean, what's going to happen to her?" Mum looked confused.

"I'm worried she's going to be bored," Amber explained. "She's not really been on her own that much, has she?"

Amber's family had got Cleo from a local cat shelter right at the beginning of the summer holidays. Amber had been desperate to get a kitten for ages, and her parents had finally agreed. Mum and Dad and her big sister, Sara, had spent ages sitting with her on the sofa, looking at the website. But as soon as Amber had seen the photo of Cleo with her brothers and sisters, Amber had known that she was the one. Amber never seen such a gorgeous cat. Cleo was a really unusual colour –

mostly ginger, but with big dark patches and huge black ears that looked like she needed to grow into them.

Amber had spent the whole holiday playing with Cleo – it was amazing how many mad games a kitten could invent to play with just a piece of string. Or a feather. Or even the flowers on Amber's flip-flops. She was going to miss Cleo so much – and she had a feeling Cleo was going to miss her, too. Even though Cleo was officially a family cat, and everyone played with her, Amber did most of the looking after. She loved feeding Cleo and making sure she always had clean water – it made her feel that the kitten was just a little bit more hers.

"She's always had me and Sara at

home to play with," Amber went on.

"I see what you mean." Mum gave her a hug. "She'll be fine, Amber. Cats are quite independent, you know. And think how much time Cleo spends snoozing! She'll just save up her playtime for when we're all home. Anyway, I'll be around some of the time – you know I only do half days. Cleo can distract me from all the marking I've got to do!"

"I suppose so," Amber agreed, a bit doubtfully. Cleo did sleep a lot. She was still only small, and she didn't seem to understand taking things easy. She'd race around until she was exhausted and then collapse in a little furry tortoiseshell heap. Amber loved it when she flumped down with her paws in the air!

She wriggled the ball out from between Cleo's paws and rolled it back down the hallway again. "I'm worried that she'll be bored and find a way to get round the front of the house. She thinks the front garden must be the most exciting thing ever, just because we won't let her go out there. She nearly escaped again yesterday, when the postman brought that parcel."

Her mum made a face. "I honestly don't think we can do much about that. We'll just have to make sure she doesn't slip out. I think the noise of the cars would put her off going on the road anyway."

Mum didn't look all that sure, though, and Amber sighed. One of their neighbours had a cat who'd been run over and badly hurt, and she hated to think of anything like that happening to Cleo. She was sure Cleo was very clever, but kittens weren't known for being sensible. If Cleo saw something interesting on the other side of the road, Amber was almost certain she'd chase after it. And it wasn't as if she could train Cleo to look both ways first.

Cleo sniffed curiously at the bags in the hallway. Today felt different. Everyone was rushing around. She whisked behind one of the rucksacks as Sara came dashing past and nearly stepped on her tail. She crouched there, watching as Amber and Sara chased up and down the stairs, looking for things they'd forgotten. Their mum was standing in the hallway, glancing at her watch.

"Come on, you two! I thought you said you'd got everything ready last night? We really do need to go – I've got a staff meeting before school."

"I'm here, I'm ready." Amber jumped down the last two steps and looked around for her bag and shoes. "I just wanted to find a photo of Cleo to show my friends. Hardly anyone's seen her yet – only Maisie and Lila when they came over."

"I'm ready, too," Sara said, sighing. "I can't believe we're going back to school – it feels as if the holidays have only just started. And everyone says Year Eight means loads more homework." Sara's secondary school wasn't that far from the house, but she usually got a lift with Mum and Amber in the mornings and walked back home with her friends.

"I shouldn't think anyone will give you much on the first day," her mum replied. "Come on. Grab your stuff and let's get in the car."

Cleo opened her mouth in a silent mew of surprise as the bag in front of her disappeared. And then she realized – the front door was open!

"Oh, Cleo, no! Sara, stop her!" Amber called out. She was all mixed up with her PE bag and rucksack and she still only had one shoe on.

Sara crouched down to try and field the kitten, but Cleo jinked expertly around her reaching hands and skipped out on to the doorstep.

Cleo caught the different outdoor smells as she leaped down the step and then darted off to investigate the wheelie bins. She'd only managed to get out into the front garden a couple of times, and she wanted to explore.

"Did you get her?" Amber came

hurrying up to her sister.

"No, she was just too speedy!" Sara gasped. "Sorry! I think she's gone behind the bins. Here, Cleo! Come on... Puss, puss!"

Mum sighed. "How does she know when we're in a hurry? Amber, can you catch her? Try not to let her go under the car – it'll take ages to get her back out again."

Amber crouched down beside the bins. The kitten was in the flower bed now, peering out through the pink geraniums.

Cleo gazed up at her with round green eyes. She didn't understand why they made such a fuss about her being *here*, when no one minded if she went through her cat flap into the back garden. She looked around, eyeing the pavement and the road beyond. There were interesting smells out there – more cats and other things, too. But the cars speeding past were so loud that she'd never dared to do more than peek round the edge of the garden wall. She wanted to, though. She was working up to it.

"There!" Amber reached through the flowers and grabbed her, and Cleo snuggled up against her school cardigan. The kitten didn't mind being caught, not really. Especially because Amber always gave her cat treats when she brought her back in.

Cleo dived out of the cat flap and shook her ears crossly. She didn't like the way it banged behind her – it always made her feel jumpy. She licked at the fur on her white front until she felt calmer and then strolled out on to the patio. The garden was very bright, and there were fat bees blundering through the lavender bush. She could even hear a bird rustling in the apple tree at the far end. But somehow the back garden didn't seem quite as exciting as it usually did.

Cleo sat on the patio, feeling the warm afternoon sun on her fur and wondering what to do. She had slept for a lot of the morning, and now she wanted to play. Amber's mum was working on her computer, and she'd stroked Cleo for a bit. But when Cleo had tried to pounce on her keyboard, she'd shooed her away. Cleo was used to playing with Amber, and she missed her. It wasn't as much fun being on her own. She could chase down the garden after that bird or wriggle into the lavender and swipe at the bees. But she never seemed to catch anything… When would Amber come back?

Then her ears flattened and she sprang up, stalking across the patio to the bench by the garden wall. Amber had gone out of the front door. Perhaps she was at the front of the house somewhere. If she hopped up on to the bench, she wouldn't be that far from the top of the wall…

Cleo wriggled her bottom and

leaped, scrambling from the arm of the bench into the twiggy mass of jasmine that was growing up the wall. She clawed and scrabbled and pulled her way up on to the top. Half her fur was standing on end and it was full of tiny green leaves, but she had done it. She was almost sure this wall led round to the front of the house, where Amber was.

Cleo paced along the top of the wall, then over the flat roof of the garage. She dropped back down on to the wall again where it ran along the side of the little front garden.

She had to pick her way carefully through the tall plants that grew up against it, but eventually she reached the front of the garden, where the wall was lower and half-hidden by bushes. She perched between the bushes, looking out on to the street.

"Cleo!"

The kitten peered curiously round the bushes and saw Amber racing down the street towards her, with her rucksack bouncing against her shoulders. Cleo stood up and purred, arching her back proudly. She'd been right! Amber *was* here! Amber would see that she'd been clever and climbed the wall. As Amber ran up to her, Cleo purred even louder and leaned down to rub her head against Amber's shoulder.

"Oh, Cleo," she murmured lovingly, "you're so naughty! How did you get out here? Mum, look!"

"Cleo!" Amber's mum stared at the kitten. "I made absolutely sure she didn't slip past me when I left to get you from school. She was in the house this afternoon – I know she was. She tried to sit on the computer while I was working."

Amber gently scooped the little kitten off the top of the wall. She held Cleo against her shoulder as Mum went to unlock the front door. "But that means she must have got round the house by herself," Amber said, looking up at the garden wall. "She can't have done… That wall's so high for her to jump up to, and then she had to get on to the garage roof!"

Cleo looked up at the wall, too, and purred smugly into Amber's ear.

Chapter Two

Now that Cleo had worked out how to climb the wall in the back garden, she was desperate to try it again. Amber had homework to do – which she thought was really unfair on her first day back. She left Cleo gobbling down her tea, hoping she would come and find her when she'd finished. But Cleo had other ideas, and when Amber's dad came home from work he was met by a purring kitten on the path.

Dad laughed as Cleo danced happily around his feet and he crouched down to fuss over her. "You're not meant to be out here, little miss. Did you slip out? Come on, then."

He opened the front door and called out, "Look who I found!"

Amber and Sara peered over the top of the stairs.

"Oh no! Was she out at the front again?" Amber hurried down to scoop Cleo up. "She's definitely learned to climb the wall, then. Mum said she must have done it earlier, but I thought Cleo might have sneaked out without her noticing. She was on the front wall when I came home!"

"She was only in the front garden." Dad looked round at Amber as he hung up his jacket. "I don't think she'll come to any harm."

"What about the road, though?" Amber sighed worriedly and then laughed as Cleo's head butted into her chin. "Oh, Cleo, are you telling me not to fuss?"

"How's Cleo?" Amber's friend Maisie asked in class a couple of days later, spotting the photo that Amber had stuck on the front of her planner. "Has she learned any more tricks?" Amber had told her about all the games she'd invented with Cleo.

Amber rolled her eyes. "Yes! She's learned how to scramble on to the back wall, then climb all the way over the garage roof so she can get into the front garden."

Lila leaned over the table. "Why? What's so exciting about your front garden?"

"Who knows?" Amber sighed. "But it's got a road in front of it, that's the problem. There's this really nice lady who lives down our street, Susan. Her cat got run over last year. He crawled back in through the cat flap with a broken leg. He had to have an operation to fix the bone back together with metal pins. Then he had to live in a cat crate for two months to stop him walking on it."

"But that's not going to happen to Cleo," Lila said comfortingly.

"It might do." Amber ran her finger over Cleo's whiskers in the photo – they were so white, and they fanned out like she had a moustache. "She's only little and she doesn't know what cars are. The people across the road are starting to have an extension built this week. Mum was telling me. She was saying it might be tricky to get out of our driveway because of all the builders' vans and things. So that's loads more traffic to worry about."

"I'm sure it will be OK..." put in a quiet voice.

Amber looked over at the other side of the table, a bit surprised. The two classes in the year had been mixed around again, and she didn't know George very well. He'd always been in the other class in her year. She'd not seen him on her way to school, either, so she guessed he didn't live very close by. They'd been on the same table for a week now, but George hadn't said much at all.

"My mum's cat, Pirate, goes up and down our street, and he does cross the road sometimes. But he's really careful. I bet your kitten will just learn what to do."

"George is right," Lila agreed. "Cats are clever. I'm sure Cleo will learn how to cross the road, no problem."

"Maybe," Amber said. She loved how Cleo was so curious – it made her even more fun to play with. But it also meant that she liked to explore everything. She sighed to herself as Mr Evans told them to stop chatting and settle down. She was probably worrying too much – it was the first time they'd had a pet, after all. She just couldn't help that little nagging feeling that Cleo was too nosy for her own good.

Cleo sat perched on the front wall, peering out from under a climbing rose and eyeing the men working on the other side of the road. There was one big truck, with a crane lifting off huge pallets of bricks. Then there were two smaller vans and lots of people going backwards and forwards between them and the house. She wanted to get closer to see what was going on.

The road was in between her and the action, though, and she didn't like the way the cars roared and growled as they shot past. Yesterday, after a few days of exploring the front garden, she'd actually ventured out on to the pavement. At first she'd just stood by the gate, flinching back when a car came past. But they all seemed to stick to the road, and she was sure the pavement looked safe enough.

She'd crept along the bottom of the wall, keeping well away from the road. Then a car had sped by. Cleo had felt the rumbling of the road under her paws and smelled the exhaust, and she'd raced back to the safety of the garden.

She still wasn't quite brave enough to cross the road and investigate the unusual things that were happening on the other side. Cleo edged between two bushes as another van came driving up. But this time when the van stopped it was on *her* side of the road.

Cleo wriggled out between the thick stems, her whiskers twitching. The driver was getting out – Cleo could see his heavy boots walking round the side of the van. Then he opened up the back doors and lifted out a box, which he carried across the road to the interesting house on the other side.

Almost without realizing it, Cleo was padding eagerly out into the middle of the pavement. The van was new and exciting, and she wanted to see what was in it.

Then the man was coming back. Cleo ducked under the sprawling fuchsia bush in the garden next door.

Amber and Sara always tried to grab her when she went out at the front of the house. She didn't want this man to catch her now and stop her exploring. But the man didn't even notice her. He just unloaded another box and set off across the road again, leaving the van's back doors open.

As Cleo edged out of the bush, she came to a sudden halt. Her collar was caught on the wiry branches. She pulled at it crossly. She hated collars.

When the safety catch came open, she tossed her head briskly from side to side, enjoying the freedom. Then she hurried out from under the bush, shaking the dry leaves from her fur.

Cleo sniffed at the tyres of the van and then stretched up, putting her front paws on the little back step. The van was full of boxes, some old sacks, a folded plastic sheet and all sorts of fascinating things. There were dark corners and good smells to investigate, too.

She jumped up, scrabbling to get her back legs on to the step, and clambered into the van. It was dusty, which made her sneeze, but that didn't put her off. She prowled further inside and rubbed up against one of the boxes. She liked this place and she wanted to mark it as hers.

Suddenly there was a shout from outside and the sound of footsteps approaching. Cleo froze, laying her ears back. What was happening? Was someone coming to chase her out? She backed between the box and a pile of sacks and watched, round-eyed, as the doors at the back of the van swung shut with a slam.

She was trapped.

Chapter Three

Amber turned to her mum, smiling in relief. "It's OK! Cleo's not in the front garden. She must have decided to stay round the back today."

Mum nodded. "Maybe the novelty's worn off."

All the same, Amber was a little bit hurt that Cleo didn't come rushing to see her as she stepped into the house.

Whenever they'd been out over the summer holidays, she'd always come to greet them. As soon as she heard the door bang, she would come dashing downstairs from Amber's room, where she'd been asleep on her bed. Or sometimes she was sitting on the living-room windowsill, watching to see them drive up.

The house felt oddly quiet and empty without a little tortoiseshell cat twirling around her feet. "Cleo!" Amber called up the stairs. "Cleo, where are you?"

Mum pushed the front door shut and looked around in surprise. "Isn't she here? She's usually desperate for us to feed her when we get in from school."

"I know..." Amber said. "Cleo! Cleo!" She hurried through to the kitchen and out into the back garden. But no kitten came galloping over the grass to meet her. The garden was empty and still, with just a few birds twittering in the trees.

Amber trailed back inside, feeling worried.

Her mum was emptying one of Cleo's pouches of kitten food into her bowl and she glanced up as Amber came in. She put down the pouch, looking thoughtful. "No sign of her?" she asked.

Amber shook her head.

"That *is* odd. Go and check upstairs, Amber. She might have got shut in one of the bedrooms."

Amber smiled. "I didn't think about that! I hope she hasn't made a mess in Sara's room. Sara got really cross when Cleo tipped over all her hairbands and stuff the other day."

She raced upstairs, but all the bedroom doors were ajar. She checked the airing cupboard on the landing, just in case, but she wasn't in there... Or in Sara's wardrobe, or hers, or Mum and Dad's. She wasn't anywhere at all.

"Mum, I don't know where she can be," Amber said, bursting back into the kitchen. She was trying very hard not to cry. Mum would only say she was getting in a state about nothing. But this really didn't feel like nothing. Cleo never missed meals.

Mum put her arm round Amber's shoulders. "Sit down for a moment, have a drink, and let's think about this." She handed Amber some squash and pushed her gently into a chair. "Cleo was around just before lunch when I went into school. And we know she's been getting more adventurous lately, going over the wall into the front garden. She's probably just gone further than before. After all, you've only been back at school a week. Cleo doesn't really know what time you come home, does she? And the fact I'm working different times of day probably confuses her, too."

"I suppose so..."

"I expect she'll be back in a minute, yowling if we don't get her food in front of her before the cat flap bangs shut."

Amber tried to laugh, but she couldn't quite manage it.

Cleo stood perched on the pile of old sacks, mewing anxiously. She didn't understand why the doors had closed so suddenly. All she knew was that now she couldn't get out. She started to pick her way carefully between the boxes back towards the doors. Perhaps when she got closer she'd find a way to escape. When she pushed on doors in the house, sometimes they opened. Although sometimes they didn't... She scampered up to the doors and scrabbled at them with her front paws. They were shut tight.

There was a growling noise and then suddenly the van lurched, and Cleo slipped over sideways with a little squeak of fright. She'd only been in a car a few times, when she was brought home from the shelter and for trips to the vet. She'd always travelled in a comfortable basket, padded with a blanket, though. She slid across the floor of the van as it pulled out into the road, meowing frantically. She hadn't meant for this to happen at all.

Cleo pressed herself into a small dark space under a storage locker that had been built for tools. It was a tight fit, but it made her feel safer. Nothing could get at her under here. She squashed herself back against the cold metal of the van's wall and waited.

Eventually the van seemed to slow down, and then it lurched to a stop.

The noisy engine was turned off, leaving Cleo's ears buzzing. There was a crunching, clashing sound, and the doors swung open. Cleo wriggled her nose out of the tiny gap and tried to see what was happening. She could smell the fresh air coming in through the open doors, and she desperately wanted to race for them. But there was so much noise. She darted back into her safe hiding place as a huge box slid past her with a shriek of metal on metal and shivered. What if more of the boxes moved as she ran for the doors? She had to try, though.

Cleo laid her ears back close to her head and crept out. With her tummy pressed against the floor of the van, she edged across to the doors.

She could see the road outside, and her whiskers twitched with the warm smells of the sunny afternoon. But just as she was getting ready to jump down, the doors clanged shut. She was trapped once more.

Cleo flung herself at the doors with a desperate wail, banging her paws against the hard metal. The doors didn't budge. She should have run for it when she could! Furious and frightened, she stomped back across the van, the fur all along her spine raised, her tail fluffed up. What was going to happen now? What if she never got out?

Miserably aware of how hungry and thirsty and lonely she felt, Cleo meowed as loudly as she could, hoping that Amber would come, the way she always did. *Surely* Amber would come and rescue her…

"Amber, I don't think she can have been hit by a car," Mum said gently, as Amber's dad came into the kitchen and hung his laptop bag over a chair. "We'd have heard. Cleo's microchipped. If she'd been taken to a vet, they would have called my mobile."

Amber had searched everywhere she could think of. She'd opened every cupboard in the house, remembering the day when Dad had accidentally shut Cleo in the cupboard under the stairs. And then she'd gone back and checked all the drawers, too. When Sara had got home from school, the sisters had gone down their road calling for her, while Mum had checked the garage and the shed. But Cleo was nowhere to be found. And what made it even worse was that Amber and Sara had found her collar under one of the bushes in front of the house next door. So now even if someone found her, they wouldn't know the number to call.

"What's up? Has Cleo disappeared?" Dad asked, giving Amber a hug. "She's probably just out exploring."

"Well, that's what I said," Mum sighed. "But it's six o'clock, Dan. She normally has her dinner about four. It's really unusual for her not to turn up for that."

"And now we've found her collar," Amber said shakily, pointing to it on the kitchen table. "So we know she was out at the front of the house. What if she's been run over?"

"No, your mum's

right. I'm sure someone would have found her and let us know, Amber." Dad frowned thoughtfully. "Maybe she is lost, though. She's only little – she could just have got confused about where she was going. How about I have another quick look along the street?"

When Dad came back a while later, he had to admit that he hadn't seen any sign of Cleo, either. As Amber picked at her dinner, she kept thinking of the open cat food pouch, which Mum had folded over and put in the fridge. Cleo must be so hungry, wherever she was.

"Try not to worry, Amber," Mum said, as she turned off Amber's light at bedtime. "She'll probably be back in the morning."

"You're not sure..."

Mum sighed. "No, I can't be *absolutely* sure. I really do think she will be, though."

Amber pulled the duvet over her head. She was desperate to sleep so that she could wake up and find Cleo stomping up and down her bed, purring and mewing until Amber got up and fed her her breakfast. But she lay awake for what seemed like hours, imagining the kitten hungry or lonely or, worst of all, hurt.

Chapter Four

Cleo woke the next morning feeling stiff and cold. She had slept on the pile of sacks, but they weren't very comfortable, not compared to her soft basket. She was also desperately hungry. She had never gone for so long without a meal – or without Amber to stroke her and fuss over her and play with her.

She sat up, shaking out her paws, and

licked at the fur on her shoulders and neck. She felt so dusty and dirty in here. But washing only made her realize how much she needed a drink of water.

Cleo froze suddenly, with one paw lifted ready to sweep over her ear – she could hear footsteps. Someone was coming! She ducked behind a large crate and watched eagerly as the van doors swung open. Hands reached into the van and a box of tools clanked down loudly. Cleo edged forward. She crept round the boxes until she was just by the doors and waited for the footsteps to move further away again. Her heart was galloping – this was her chance!

Cleo jumped down on to the road and scurried under the van. She needed to stop and think about what to do next. She had hoped that once she was out of the van she would see her house, her garden wall and maybe even Amber. Although she knew that the van had moved, it had no windows in the back, and she didn't really understand that it had travelled from one place to another. So she was deeply confused when she realized that she was somewhere different – somewhere that did not smell familiar at all. Cleo peered out from round the back wheel of the van, looking up and down the road. She was lost.

Amber waved goodbye to Mum reluctantly and slung her rucksack over her shoulder. Lila came running up as she trailed into the playground.

"Are you all right?" Lila said anxiously. "Your eyes are all red. Amber, what's the matter?"

"It's Cleo," Amber sniffed. "She never came home for her tea last night. Mum and Dad said they were sure she'd be back when we got up, but she wasn't!" She swallowed hard. "I didn't want to come to school. I wanted to stay at home and keep looking for her. Mum said she's going to ring all the vets this morning. That's in case … in case she's been brought in because she's had an accident."

"Oh no," Lila whispered. "But you were saying only yesterday that you were worried about her being run over."

"I know!" Amber pressed her hands into her eyes. She didn't want to start crying again, not at school. "That makes it worse," she whispered. "I feel like I made it happen by worrying about it."

Lila put an arm round her shoulders. "Of course you didn't," she said firmly. "All it means is that you were sensible to worry. And you don't know that anything bad's happened! She might just be shut in somebody's garage."

"I guess so," Amber muttered.

Then Maisie came hurrying up, and Amber stared down at her shoes as

Lila whispered what had happened. She didn't want to hear her friends talking about it – it only made Cleo's disappearance seem more real.

"Did you go looking for her?" Maisie asked.

"Down the whole street. And Dad asked some of the neighbours when he got home last night. If Cleo isn't back by this afternoon, we're going to put posters up."

Lila made a face. "I hate those posters. They're so sad. But I bet they work," she added hurriedly.

"There's the bell." Maisie squeezed

Amber's hand. "Are you going to be OK? Do you want us to say something to Mr Evans for you?"

Amber shook her head, horrified. Imagine her teacher making a fuss and the whole class knowing. "I'll be fine. Please don't tell anyone, Maisie. I just don't want to talk about Cleo – it's making me feel too miserable."

After school, Amber dashed out to find her mum, hoping that she'd have good news. But she could tell as soon as she saw Mum on the other side of the playground that she didn't. She looked worried, even though she smiled at Amber and held out her arms for a hug.

"She hasn't come home, has she?" Amber asked, her voice muffled in her mum's jacket.

"Not yet, sweetie."

Amber swallowed. It felt like her heart was swelling up and blocking her throat. "Let's go home," she told Mum, and her voice sounded odd, even to her. "We need to start on the Lost Cat posters. I'll find a good photo of Cleo."

"Yes, I suppose we should," Mum agreed. "I really did think she'd have turned up by now. I wonder if she's shut in somewhere."

"Where?" Amber turned to look at Mum.

"Someone's shed, maybe? You know how nosy Cleo is. If she found one open she'd definitely pop in for a look around. And then maybe the person came back and shut the door without seeing her."

Amber nodded. "Oh, yes! I'll put that on the poster, then. We'll ask if people can look in their sheds. And Lila said she could be shut in a garage. I wonder if there's anywhere else..."

As soon as she got home, Amber raced upstairs to find the laptop she shared with Sara. Normally they argued about whose turn it was to have it, but Amber knew that today Sara wouldn't mind if she got it out of her bedroom. She carried it into her own room and started to work out what the poster should say.

"Amber?"

Amber gazed up at Sara in the doorway. "Look!" she sniffed, holding out the laptop to her big sister. There were tears dripping down her nose.

"Oh…" Sara sat down next to Amber on the bed, peering over at the photo on the screen. "I took that one on Mum's mobile. Cleo thought the phone was something she could eat – that's why she's so close up. She looks really cute."

"I bet she's really scared, wherever she is," Amber sobbed. "She's not going to understand what's going on, is she? She won't even know we're looking for her."

"I bet she will," Sara said. "She knows we love her, Amber. I'll help you put the posters up, and she'll be home soon. It'll be OK."

Once she'd darted out from under the van on to the pavement, Cleo squirmed under the nearest gate. She still had no idea where she was and why she couldn't find her way home to Amber, but she was so thirsty. She had to find something to drink.

She followed her nose down the pathway at the side of the house and came out into the back garden. She could smell water, she was sure. There was a delicate pattering sound and she hurried towards it. She was right – there was a huge bowl full of water, with a little fountain in the middle.

Cleo put her paws up on the edge and drank greedily. It tasted odd, not like the water from her bowl at home, but it was still good. She liked the fountain too, and she darted her head about, trying to catch the water drops in her mouth. They got on her ears and her whiskers, but she didn't mind – it helped to get rid of the dusty feeling.

Cleo padded across the garden, sniffing for something to eat – she felt much hungrier, now that she wasn't so thirsty. There was a definite smell of at least one other cat around, but none appeared.

Eventually she came to a little teepee set up on the grass. She peered around the tent flap, sniffing hopefully. There on a rug was a plastic plate, with half a stale sandwich on it. Cleo darted in and gobbled down the sandwich, which was full of dry cheese. It was delicious! She was still hungry, so she washed herself thoroughly all over, making sure she got every last crumb out of her whiskers.

Then she yawned and curled up on

the bit of the rug that was in the sun. The garden was quiet and felt safe, and the September sun was very warm. Before long Cleo was fast asleep.

She was woken mid-afternoon by a sudden noise – a loud wailing. Panicked, Cleo whisked round to the other side of the tent and hid behind it, peering out to see what was going on.

A boy came out of the back door of the house, carrying a plate. He wasn't the one making the noise – that seemed to be coming from inside. The boy wandered to the end of the garden and sat down on a swing beside the tent. He swung idly back and forth, nibbling at the sandwich. He was staring vaguely round the garden when he spotted Cleo.

He stopped swinging at once, and Cleo froze.

The boy slipped off the swing, leaving the sandwich on the grass and crept towards the tent.

"Here, puss, puss…" he called.

Cleo shrunk back behind the tent, as the wailing started up again.

The boy glanced towards the house. "Is that noise scary? It's just my little brother throwing a wobbly."

Cleo could tell from the boy's voice that he was friendly. And he had another of those sandwiches. Cleo came a little way out and eyed him hopefully.

"I haven't seen you before," the boy murmured. "I wonder who's got a new kitten? You haven't got a collar on, have you?" He looked carefully at the kitten's neck. "Nope, no collar. Hey, where are you going? Oh!" He laughed. The kitten was hurrying over the grass towards his abandoned sandwich. "Do you want it? Oh, wow, you do."

Cleo was already tearing at the corner of the sandwich, gulping it down greedily.

"You're starving!" The boy smiled slowly as he watched the sandwich disappear. "Maybe you're a stray?"

He grinned as the kitten devoured the last bit of sandwich and sniffed the plate all over to see if she'd missed any.

"Who do you belong to, hey? What's your name?" He reached out to tickle Cleo gently behind the ears. "I reckon you look like a … umm. Maybe a Smudge? With that dark splodge over your eye? But you look like a girl cat to me. Smudge doesn't sound like a girl. What about Patch? Are you called

Patch? That's why my mum called our cat Pirate, you know. Because he's got an eyepatch."

"George! George!"

Cleo darted away behind the tent again, and the boy sighed. "There's Mum. I'll come back later with some more food for you. That's if you're still here..."

Chapter Five

Amber followed Sara back into the house, trying to feel hopeful. They had put up posters all along their street and the streets close by. Then they'd gone into the little convenience store at the end of their road and asked if they could put up one on their notice board. But it still didn't feel like enough. Amber couldn't just sit in the house, waiting for Cleo to come home. She needed to be doing something.

Perhaps she could go and ask some of their neighbours who had sheds and garages if she could check them. Then her eyes widened – she'd just thought of another place where Cleo could have got trapped. The family across the road was having a lot of work done on their house and had moved in with their grandparents for a few weeks. Jan, their mum, had told Amber's mum that they'd have to pack everything up in boxes. But that meant some of the rooms were closed up, and there were piles of stuff everywhere – all sorts of places where a kitten could get shut in.

Amber was so excited, and so sure

she was right, that she didn't even stop to ask Mum or Sara to go with her. She'd just have time to catch the builders before they went home, she reckoned. She slipped back out of the front door and crossed the road. Mum would tell her off, but if she came back with Cleo, surely Mum wouldn't mind that much… And Amber was certain she would bring her back.

She hesitated outside number 22, looking for one of the builders to ask. Until now, every time they'd gone past there had been someone around, unloading stuff from vans or hoisting materials up on to the scaffolding. But now there was no one at all.

"Hello?" Amber called, stepping on to the driveway.

No one came. Amber clenched her fists. She just couldn't wait any longer. What if Cleo was starving? She knew it was stupid – and she'd get into trouble if Mum and Dad found out she'd gone into Jan's garden with all the building going on. But she had to!

She walked up to the house and tried to peer in through the front windows, pressing her nose against the glass. She was trying so hard to see through the dusty panes that she didn't hear one of the builders coming round the side of the house.

"Just what exactly do you think you're doing?"

Amber swung round to find a tall man staring down at her. He was covered in dust. The greyish colour made him look like a statue. "I'm – I'm looking for my kitten," she squeaked.

"Your *kitten*?"

"She's gone missing. I thought she might have got shut in…" Amber's voice trailed away – the man looked so cross.

"You shouldn't be here. Don't you realize how dangerous it is, messing around on a building site?"

Amber hung her head, tears filling her eyes. Then she looked up again, straightening her shoulders. This was too important to let go. "But she's been gone a whole day. What if she's got trapped somewhere? Jan said some of the rooms were shut up to keep the dust out – what if she's in one of them?"

"They've all been closed up since we started," the man said, more gently. "And we'd have heard her mewing, wouldn't we?"

Amber's head drooped again. "Maybe… I really thought she had to be here. I'm so worried about her."

"I'll keep an eye out for her," the man told Amber. "What colour is she?"

"She's a tortoiseshell, mostly gingery with black patches. We live just there." Amber pointed across the road.

"All right. Now, out of here, and don't even think of coming back. What if something had fallen off the scaffolding?"

Amber nodded, her eyes widening. She hurried out of the garden and crossed the road, her cheeks burning. That had been awful. But at least the builder hadn't insisted on coming back home with her and telling Mum.

George slid back through the kitchen, glad that his mum was still occupied sorting out Toby, his little brother. Everyone said that Toby was going through a stage, or that it was the terrible twos, but it basically meant that he was either really, really happy or furious and never anything in between. Right now it meant that Mum wasn't going to notice him sneaking his leftover packed lunch outside to the kitten.

George checked – yes, there was quite a bit of his lunch left. He didn't think the kitten would be keen on grapes, but she would definitely be up for cocktail sausages, he decided. Pirate was always trying to nick them when Mum was making his packed lunch.

He hurried back down the garden, hoping that the kitten would still be there. *Perhaps I should really be hoping that she's gone home*, George thought to himself, feeling a bit guilty. The little kitten was probably still not used to being out much.

Then he saw her peeping at him from behind the tent again and forgot to worry about her owner.

As soon as Cleo saw the boy, she darted out from her hiding place at once and came up quite close. Maybe he had more food. She still felt so hungry, even after both those sandwiches. She was used to two good meals and the odd snack of cat treats from Amber. She stopped a short distance away and sniffed at the lunchbox as George put it down on the grass.

George held out a sausage on the palm of his hand and looked hopefully at the kitten. Then he laughed as the little cat dived at him and started nibbling the sausage straight out of his hand. Her mouth was so soft, and her damp nose nuzzled at George's fingers.

"You're really nice," he whispered, using his not-sausagey hand to stroke the kitten's soft back.

The kitten finished off the sausage and looked hopefully into the lunchbox for more. She snagged the last sausage out of the little pot, and it disappeared in seconds.

"Don't make yourself sick," George told her. "Sorry, that's the last one. There's still a bit of cheese, though." He took it out and pulled off the cling film. "There you go." He watched, smiling, as the kitten ate the cheese, too, and then sat down quite heavily and began to wash her ears and face. Her stomach looked a lot rounder than it had ten minutes ago.

"I wish I knew where you'd come from, Patch," George murmured. "I probably shouldn't have given you all that food, if you're just going to go home for your tea. But you looked starving, the way you wolfed down that sandwich."

The kitten licked her bright pink tongue over her nose and then looked at the boy with gleaming golden eyes. She got up and padded a little closer.

George gazed down in surprise – he'd thought maybe the kitten would hurry away once the food had all gone. But instead she clambered on to George's lap and slumped down, clearly exhausted by so much eating. She yawned, and then she seemed to melt into the space on George's lap, completely saggy, like a beanbag toy. She was asleep.

Chapter Six

Cleo padded up to the shed and wriggled through a small gap in the boards. She gazed around, hoping to find something else to eat. The boy, George, had left her some food there in the morning – toast crusts and the end of a boiled egg. It wasn't like anything Cleo had eaten before, but she'd quite enjoyed it. She was feeling

hungry again now, though.

George had shown her this place the evening before. He'd opened the door and gone in to shake the dust and spiders' webs off some cushions from the garden chairs. He had arranged them into a comfy pile for a bed and filled an old plant saucer from the outside tap with water. He'd even brought Cleo a fish finger. It was a bit fluffy from being in his pocket, but she hadn't cared. Then he'd shown Cleo that there was a hole in the shed wall, just big enough for a kitten to squeeze in and out of.

Cleo had spent the night curled up on the cushions, but she kept startling awake. It wasn't like being in a house. There were strange noises, and they seemed so close with just the thin wooden walls of the shed to protect her. Squeaks and chirrups and rustlings in the trees and the flowerbeds, and once, horribly close, a great deep sniff. Cleo had frozen, watching the little hole in the shed wall. After the sniff there had been a pause, a terrifying silence while she'd wondered if the creature was going to claw its way in. But it had gone away, obviously deciding that Cleo wasn't worth the effort. It had left behind a sharp, unmistakeable whiff of something wild, and hungry.

She had spent the day exploring the garden – every so often coming up against that smell again. She could still catch a trace of it now…

Cleo hated the thought of spending another night in the shed, with that creature so close by. As kind as George was, she needed to find her home, where she slept indoors on Amber's bed or occasionally in her basket. She wanted Amber to snuggle up against. She clambered back out of the shed then crept uncertainly past the house, down the side passage and out into George's front garden. There she looked out on to the street, wondering how to get home. It was mid-afternoon and quite quiet, even though there were children's voices in the distance, returning home from school. Cleo peered down the road hopefully, wondering if one of them was Amber, coming to find her. But the voices didn't sound right.

Cleo hopped up on to the wall, so she could look around from a high point. The street stretched out in front of her – grey and empty, and utterly unfamiliar. Which way should she go?

She sniffed the air, trying to catch a scent of home, but there was nothing. At last she jumped down from the wall and set off down the street, making for a garden with straggly bushes spilling out on to the pavement. She would go in short hops, from hiding place to hiding place, she decided. In case that creature was still around.

A strange rattling sound suddenly came around the corner of the road, and Cleo scuttled towards the bushes and ducked underneath. There was a loud clattering and then footsteps. A face appeared under the branches, and Cleo's heart slowed a little. It was the boy who had looked after her.

"What are you doing?" George muttered. "You shouldn't be out on the pavement – I bet you don't understand about cars."

He thought of Amber at school, worrying about her kitten getting run over. He ought to ask her if the kitten had been out in her front garden again. She'd been really quiet at school today, not at all chatty like she usually was.

He scooped Cleo up and snuggled her with one arm, glancing back over his shoulder. His mum hadn't got round the corner yet – Toby was throwing a strop about being in the pushchair.

"Don't wriggle too much," George warned. "It's tricky scooting with only one hand."

He whooshed the last few metres towards his house and shoved his scooter into the little shelter down the side passage. The man next door, Luke, had helped Dad build it for all their bikes and things. The kitten was wriggling more and more. "I know," he whispered. "I'm just waiting for Mum to open the door. Here, look!" He slipped his rucksack off his shoulders and crouched down, bringing out his lunchbox.

The kitten stopped struggling at once and pricked her ears forward.

"I saved you some of my lunch," George told her. "You like cheese, don't you?" He held out a cheese cube to the kitten, who swallowed it almost whole and then tried to burrow into the lunchbox to get more. George giggled. "You really do like cheese..." He peered round the corner of the side passage. "Just putting my scooter away, Mum!"

"All right. Close the front door when you come in," his mum called back. "Come on, Toby. We're home now."

"You see," George whispered. "Mum's still busy with my brother. She isn't going to notice if I sneak you up to my room, is she? You'll be safe up there, Patch. No more going near the road."

He picked up the lunchbox again, then hurried in through the front door and slipped upstairs.

"Can I make some leaflets about Cleo, Mum?" Amber asked, as she undid her school shoes. "Maisie suggested it. We could put them through people's doors, in case they didn't see the posters."

"I suppose it could encourage the neighbours to look in their sheds and garages," Mum agreed. "But you're not to go out delivering them without me or Sara," she added with a stern look.

Mum had been really cross the day

before, when Amber had come back in after going to the house across the road. Luckily, Amber hadn't had to explain exactly where she had been – she'd just said that she'd gone out looking for Cleo.

Amber opened up the laptop and started to write the leaflet. She dropped in the photo of Cleo and added a message asking people to check their sheds and garages, then put her mum's phone number at the bottom. Then she printed them out and went into the kitchen to show Mum.

"Do you want to go and deliver them now?" Mum asked. "I've got some time before I make dinner."

"Please." Amber hugged her. "Look, I've made enough for our road and

Bramble Crescent. Cleo could have easily gone round into their gardens."

Mum nodded and got out her phone. "I'll just text Sara to tell her where we are."

They set off down their road, taking turns to post the leaflets. It was surprisingly hard to push the flimsy sheets of paper through the letterboxes, and Amber hoped they wouldn't just get squashed inside and missed.

They were halfway back down the other side of the road when Amber noticed that the builder who'd told her off was coming out of Jan's house. She stopped, staring at him in panic. What if he told Mum about yesterday? Mum would be so cross. She posted the next few leaflets extra-slowly, hoping that he'd go back inside before they reached him. But he didn't.

As they approached the house, Amber lurked behind Mum. Maybe the builder would think that this was another family looking for their lost cat. But she was pretty sure he knew exactly who she was.

"Hello!" Mum smiled at him. "We're from across the road. Our kitten's gone missing. Can I give you one of these, just in case you spot her? It's got my number on. She's been gone a couple of days now. Amber here's really missing her."

Amber's eyes widened in panic. Now he was bound to say something…

"Of course," the builder said. "Do you want to hand me a couple more? I can give them to the other guys. I'm Luke, by the way." He smiled at Amber, and she wasn't sure, but she thought he gave her just a hint of a wink, as if to say he'd keep her secret.

Chapter Seven

"This is my bedroom," George explained to the kitten. Then he laughed to himself. "I know you don't really understand a word I say," he murmured. "You're more bothered about the cheese than anything else, aren't you? Here…" He grabbed a piece of paper from his desk and used it like a plate for his leftover sandwich.

"I can't keep on giving you sandwiches," he said. "It can't be good for you to be living on my leftovers. But Mum would have seen me if I got you some of Pirate's cat food."

He sat there watching the kitten nibble her way through the sandwich. He hadn't thought about keeping the kitten before. But could he? Of course the kitten might have a proper home where someone wanted her, even if she didn't have a collar. Some cats just wouldn't wear them. Pirate was an expert at taking them off – or he had been. They used to have to go on collar hunts in the garden, but Pirate didn't go out much any more. He was fourteen, and his legs hurt. He spent most of his days asleep on someone's bed. George really loved him, but Pirate had always seemed more like Mum's cat. He didn't play with George that much. Not like this bouncy little kitten… She could be his very own.

"You've been in my garden a whole day now," George pointed out. "At least, I think you have. And you haven't tried to go home. Do you like it better here, Patch, hmm?" But that didn't mean the kitten hadn't got an owner… Maybe she was just good at losing collars, too. George sighed.

She didn't really look like she had been living as a stray for a long time. She wasn't skinny or grubby-looking. "I expect someone's looking for you," he admitted. "Well, if you were mine, I'd be making a lot more effort to find you. I reckon you'd be better off with me."

The kitten gazed around George's bedroom with interest and padded over to investigate his bookcase. She gazed up at it, wriggled her bottom a bit and made a flying leap up to the top. Then she stood there looking proud of herself.

Cleo sniffed at George's Lego spaceship, and the fur rose a little along her spine. She liked this house, and she liked the boy. But there was something wrong. Cleo hadn't shared a home with another cat since she left the shelter where she'd lived with her mother and the rest of her litter, but she was almost sure there was another cat here. That this house *belonged* to another cat. And perhaps the boy belonged to the other cat, too.

She nosed at the spaceship again, leaping back a little as it slid away on its wheels, and the boy leaped to catch it. Then Cleo jumped down again and wandered over to George's bed. The other-cat smell was even stronger here. She backed away from the bed, her tail twitching nervously.

Just then the bedroom door swung open and the boy jumped. "Oh, Pirate, it's only you! I thought it was Mum. Hey, don't be like that..."

A huge black-and-white cat stood in the doorway, glaring at Cleo. His fat black tail was slowly fluffing up, getting even fatter as every hair stood on end. Pirate hissed, lowering his head to stare Cleo in the eyes.

Cleo felt her own fur rising up and she hissed, too – a thin, feeble noise compared to the sound the larger cat was making.

"Oh no," George muttered. The kitten was crouched by his bed, looking terrified – but her tail was switching from side to side in just the same angry way that Pirate's was.

"Pirate, she's just a kitten." He got up and tried to shoo Pirate out of his room, but Pirate wasn't having any of it. He swerved round George and jumped at the smaller cat, sending her flying with a fat paw.

"No!" George yelled, panicking. He'd never expected this to happen. Pirate was so slow and sleepy, but now it was like he'd got ten years younger. Pirate was massive compared to the kitten – what if he really hurt the little thing? George reached down, trying to grab the kitten. He'd go and put her in the garden and shut Pirate in. But then he jumped back with a yelp. He'd got in between Pirate and the kitten, and there were claw marks all down the back of his hand, oozing thin red lines of blood.

George looked miserably at Pirate – he'd never seen him look so furious. But he supposed he should have realized. This was Pirate's house, and another cat had suddenly turned up. Pirate was right to be hissing and spitting and clawing. Then he gasped as Pirate launched himself at the kitten, bowling her over with a swipe from his huge paw.

Cleo squealed in fright. This was nothing like the play fights she'd had with her brothers and sisters back at the shelter, and she didn't know what to do. She made a desperate leap, scrabbling on to the windowsill.

Pirate sat below, staring up at Cleo, still making those horrible hissing sounds – but he couldn't easily jump to that height any more.

Cleo didn't know that, though. The window was only open a crack, but she just managed to shoot through the gap before George could grab her.

"Come back!" George wailed. His bedroom was at the side of the house, and the window looked out on to the two garages – theirs and next door's. The kitten was teetering on the narrow windowsill.

"Come on, here, puss," George called. He was trying to sound calm and coaxing, but his voice was trembling. The kitten hissed at him and jumped down on to the steeply sloping garage roof. She clung to the tiles, her fur all fluffed up and her eyes round with fear.

George raced out of his bedroom and almost crashed into his mum on the landing.

"George? What's going on? What was all that noise? Are you teasing Pirate?"

"No! I'll explain in a minute." He dodged past his mum, tore down the stairs and out of the front door.

"Please come down," George whispered, gazing up at the kitten. "I really don't want you to fall."

His mum appeared at the door,

looking really cross. "George! What is going on? Get back in here!"

"I can't, Mum. Look…" He pointed up at the kitten, and his mum came over to see.

"Oh!" Mum cried. "Whose kitten is that?"

"I don't know. But she's stuck on the roof." George felt bad not explaining how the kitten had got on to the roof in the first place, but he hadn't exactly told his mum a lie…

"How on earth are we going to get it down?" Mum said. "Poor little thing – it looks terrified!"

"Kitty!" Toby clambered down the front step and pointed up at the kitten.

Mum caught his hand quickly. "Yes, it is. But the kitty's stuck, Toby. Shh, now, don't scare it."

"Mum, what are we going to do?" George whispered.

"Pirate!" His mum gasped, pointing up at George's window. "How did he get up there?"

George craned his neck to look

up at the window. He could just see Pirate's black-and-white face, pressed up against the opening. But Pirate was too big to squeeze through the way the kitten had. He just stood there, yowling.

Cleo could see him, too. The older cat looked enormous, and she was sure it was about to leap out of the window after her. She backed away, hissing, but her claws slipped on the tiles, and she slid even further down the steep roof with a terrified mew.

Mum turned to George. "We need a ladder. There's one in the shed – at least, I think there is... Stay here with Toby and try to calm the kitten down. First I'm going to get Pirate off there before he hurts himself or frightens the little one even more." She pushed Toby's hand into George's and disappeared inside.

George looked up at the kitten clinging desperately on to the roof and felt so guilty. He should never have brought her into the house.

"Just hold on," he called softly. "It's going to be OK. We'll get you down. And then I promise we'll try and find who you really belong to."

Chapter Eight

"Are you all right?" said a man's voice from behind George.

George whirled round. It was Luke from next door. George hadn't even heard his van drive up. "Hi!" he said breathlessly. "Do you have a ladder in your van? Mum's gone to look for one, but she's not sure where it is."

"What do you need a ladder... Oh,

I see." Luke peered up at the kitten clinging to the garage roof. "Hold on a sec." He hurried back to his van.

George went back to murmuring nonsense to the kitten and trying to stop Toby from climbing up the drainpipe to get to her. He glanced up at his bedroom. Mum must have grabbed Pirate and put him somewhere safe, because now his window was wide open. Maybe Mum thought the kitten could jump back in. But George was pretty sure such a little cat couldn't jump up there from the steep roof, not without sliding back down again.

"I've shut Pirate in the kitchen," said his mum, rushing out. "But I can't find the ladder, I think it must be in the garage."

"It's OK." George pointed to Luke, who was coming up the path with a stepladder. "Luke's got one."

His mum gave a huge sigh of relief. "Hi, Luke. You turned up just at the right time. I've got a bag of cat treats. I was thinking we could try and coax the kitten back up to the window with them, but it'll definitely be easier this way."

Luke unfolded the ladder and slowly moved it towards the garage. "I don't want to scare it away," he said. "Pass me some of those treats."

Mum emptied a few into his hand and he climbed up the ladder, holding out the treats towards the kitten. "Come on, puss. Here, look. Don't you want them?"

Cleo hissed feebly at the strange man.

She was so frightened she didn't know what to do – she could only cling on.

George watched, his heart thumping. What if Luke couldn't reach? Or the kitten tried to dodge him and fell?

"Hold the ladder, can you?" Luke called down quietly to George's mum. "I need both hands… Aha! Got you." The kitten wriggled in his arms as he climbed back down the ladder one-handed. "There we are. You're safe now. Yes, you eat those."

He laughed as Cleo sniffed out the cat treats at last, leaning over to nuzzle eagerly at the bag in George's mum's hand. "Well, it doesn't look like she's come to any harm, does it?" He peered at Cleo's black and white and ginger coat, frowning. "I wonder… But it's too far, surely. Here, can you hold her a minute?" Luke passed the kitten to George and dug in his pocket. "Would you say she looks like that?" He held out a slip of paper, with a little photo of a kitten on it.

"Yes," George's mum said, looking at the leaflet. "I think so..."

"I don't believe it." Luke shook his head. "Well, that girl who lives opposite the house I'm working on is going to be pleased, if this really is her. Are you Cleo, hey?"

"Cleo!" George gasped. He stared at the kitten. "*Amber's* Cleo?"

Luke looked thoughtful. "I think her mum did say she was

called Amber. She's got red hair?"

"That's her! This is Amber's cat? She's in my class. So that's why she's been looking so upset." He looked down at Cleo, his cheeks reddening. He'd wanted to steal Amber's kitten! "But how did she get all the way over here?" he asked suddenly. "Amber told me she lives on the other side of town, by the adventure playground."

Luke made a face and nodded towards the van. "Well, guess where that's been parked. Right outside her house."

"Amber did say her kitten was really nosy," George said. "She was worried about her getting run over, because she'd started going out on to the street."

"You think she got into your van?" George's mum said in surprise, shaking out a few more cat treats and feeding them to Cleo.

"She must have done. I'd better take her home," Luke sighed. "And apologize for catnapping her."

"You didn't mean to!" George's mum laughed. "I'm sure they'll just be delighted to have her back. Do you want to borrow Pirate's cat carrier? The poor kitten probably won't like it much, it'll smell of Pirate, but you'll need to put her in something."

"Before she eats all the cat treats and makes a getaway!" Luke agreed.

"Can I come with you?" George asked shyly. "I won't get in the way or anything. I'd just like to help take her home."

"If it's OK with your mum. You can

sit in the front with me and hold the carrier. I don't want it wobbling about."

"Of course you can," Mum said. "Hold on a minute and I'll get it out of the garage."

George smiled. He could imagine how pleased Amber was going to be. If he'd lost Pirate, he'd have been in a real state.

"Amber, can you get the door?" Mum called. "I've got crumble mix all over my hands."

Amber put down the jingly ball she'd found under the shoe rack, blinking away her tears. She kept wanting to cry – everything in the house seemed to remind her of Cleo.

"If it's those window people again, just say no thank you," her mum added.

Amber's mum really didn't like people trying to sell her double-glazing, and they always turned up when she was cooking the dinner. Amber opened the front door, rehearsing a polite go-away smile.

"Oh!" It was the builder from across the road. Amber bit at her bottom lip. What if he was coming to tell Mum on her, after all? But he was smiling.

"I've brought you a present. Me and my friend here." He stepped back so that Amber could see the boy beside him, who was holding a plastic cat carrier.

"George?" Amber stared at her classmate for a moment – then she looked down at the cat carrier, and her eyes went wide with hope. "Have you… Have you—?"

"Is it her?" George asked anxiously. "We thought it must be."

Cleo scrabbled madly at the sides of the carrier, mewing and mewing. Amber was there! The boy had brought her back to Amber. Why wouldn't they let her out?

"Amber, what is it?" Amber's mum came up the hallway, drying her hands on a tea towel. "Luke, hello. Is there a problem over the road?"

"Mum, they've found Cleo! Thank you so much!" Amber pulled open the latch and reached in to stroke the kitten. "I thought you'd never come home..." she murmured, lifting her out and snuggling Cleo against her shoulder.

"Where was she?" she asked.

"I found her in my garden," George explained. "But I didn't know she was yours. I, um, fed her my leftovers," he admitted. "And then she got stuck on our garage roof, and Luke helped to get her down." He couldn't bring himself to tell Amber that he'd lured her kitten into his house and got her into a fight with Pirate.

But Amber beamed at him. "Thank you for feeding her. I was so worried she was going to be starving!"

"I reckon she went for a ride in the back of my van," Luke put in. "I can't see how else she turned up in our neighbourhood. It's a good couple of miles away."

"Goodness," Amber's mum said.

"She stowed away! I'll have to ring Sara and Dad and tell them. You don't know how relieved they'll be. We were imagining the worst things…"

"I'm glad I found her," George said to Amber.

"Not as glad as I am," Amber said, giggling as Cleo licked her chin. "You couldn't be."

"You know a lot about cats," Amber said admiringly, watching George tickle Cleo on just the right spot behind her ear. She'd invited George round to tea to say thank you – and to let him see how Cleo was. He'd asked Amber about her at school a few times, and she thought George must have really liked the kitten.

"Our cat's called Pirate, because he looks like he has an eye patch. He's my mum's actually. She got him before I was born."

"So he's pretty old then?"

"Uh-huh. He's a bit slow now – he doesn't race around like this one does. But he's still special," George added firmly.

It was true. Pirate might be slow and not that good at chasing toys, but he almost always slept on George's feet at night. Mum had told him the other night that Pirate had done that since George was a baby. She and Dad had tried to keep him away because they were worried that Pirate might hurt him by accident. But Pirate wouldn't be shooed away – and he was the best one for stopping baby George crying. "In the end we gave up," his mum had said, smiling down at Pirate, who was sitting between them. "He'd obviously decided you were his, you see."

George watched Cleo clamber up into Amber's lap and flop down, purring. He stroked her ears, and nodded to himself. Amber was Cleo's, and he belonged to Pirate – and that was exactly the way it should be.

The Homeless Kitten

For everyone who has adopted a cat or kitten from a shelter – you are fabulous!

Chapter One

"You're coming with me, Lily? Are you sure?" Dad grinned at her, widening his eyes and pretending to be shocked.

"I like the sound of a walk with you and Hugo in the woods. It'll be nice and cool under the trees. Anyway –" Lily made a face back at him – "I'd come with you more often if you didn't go so fast. You've both got really long legs and I haven't." Lily reached down to rub the dog's soft creamy white ears. "Yes, you do, don't you? Great big long legs." She looked up at Dad. "You're not planning on one of your five-mile hikes, are you?" she asked suspiciously.

Dad laughed. "No, not in this weather – it's too hot for a long walk now. Anyway, I took Hugo out running with me early this morning."

Lily nodded. Hugo needed loads of exercise. Dad took him for at least two long walks every day and he usually went for a quick walk in the park with Mum when she stopped working to take a lunch break. At weekends Dad often took Hugo in the car to the hills just outside town for a really good run. Lily's big sister, Carly, loved to go with them but Lily wasn't so keen. It always seemed to rain when she went on one of Dad's big days out.

Hugo was mostly German Shepherd – nobody was quite sure what else. Carly had told her that German Shepherds were originally bred from dogs trained to guard flocks of sheep from wolves and bears. They were used to working hard. Dad had wanted a really energetic dog and he'd fallen in love with Hugo at the animal shelter. He was so unusual with his white coat. The shelter staff said that Hugo had got too big for his elderly owner to look after properly – and at the time he hadn't even stopped growing.

Mum and Dad had explained to Lily and Carly that they'd have to be really gentle with him as he was a rescue dog, and because white German Shepherds could be quite sensitive and nervous. They were no good as pets for people who were out at work all day – if they were left alone they could end up wrecking a house because they were so miserable! Luckily, Mum worked at home as a graphic designer so Hugo was never by himself for long.

"Is Carly coming?" Dad asked. "Shout up the stairs for her, Lily."

"No, Mum's taking her round to Maisie's house in a minute. Maisie's got one of those giant paddling pools in her garden." Lily sighed enviously. It was the first week of the summer holidays and the weather was already so hot.

Even though it was sweltering, Hugo was still keen for his walk. He was standing by the front door staring at them both, his gleaming blue eyes hopeful. One of the boys in Carly's class had told her that Hugo was a spooky wolf dog because of his white coat and blue eyes, and Carly had got into trouble for chasing the boy round the playground. She adored Hugo even more than Dad did and Hugo loved her to bits.

Dad clipped on Hugo's lead and opened the front door. Hugo pulled Dad eagerly down the path, keen to be off, and Lily quickly slipped on her trainers and hurried after them. "Bye, Mum! See you later, Carly!"

As they turned out of the gate, Hugo suddenly stiffened, his ears pricking forward and his tail flicking from side to side.

Dad peered over the fence, where Hugo was looking. "What are you so excited about? Oh! No, Hugo, no chasing cats."

"Is it Pixie?" Lily ran down the path to look. "Hello, sweetheart!" Pixie was a gorgeous silvery tabby cat who belonged to their next-door neighbour, Anna. Lily loved to play with Pixie – so much that Carly was always teasing her about it. Everyone else in the family preferred dogs but Lily's room was full of cat posters and cat books… Even her pyjamas had kittens on them.

Luckily for Lily, Pixie was always popping into their garden. Sometimes she even walked along the garden wall, and then hopped on to the garage roof and in through Lily's bedroom window. Lily loved to pretend that Pixie was hers but Mum always shooed the cat out whenever she saw her. She said it wasn't fair on Hugo, letting a cat into his house.

Now the tabby cat was perched on the fence, looking down disapprovingly at Hugo, her tail swishing. Hugo had never chased Pixie but Lily thought he secretly wanted to. He didn't like her walking across his garden. He always stared at her out of the long windows in the living room, his nose pressed up against the glass. If Pixie hung around for too long, Hugo would let out a series of mighty barks.

Pixie rubbed her head against Lily's cheek, glared at Hugo and jumped back down to the other side of the fence. Hugo barked and wagged his tail excitedly.

"Come on, boy," Dad said gently. "Walk time. Off to the woods."

Hugo shook himself and loped out on to the pavement, Dad and Lily jogging after him. The little woods they were going to weren't far away – just a short walk up the hill.

"Ohhh, that's nice." Lily sighed happily, lifting her hair up off the back of her neck as they walked under the trees. "It's so much cooler here in the shade. Look, Hugo likes it, too. He must be so hot with all that thick fur."

Dad nodded. "I think this is one of Hugo's favourite places. So many good smells and all those squirrels."

"And sticks." Lily grinned. Hugo loved it when they threw sticks for him to chase after. "Are you going to let him off the lead?"

Dad looked around thoughtfully. Hugo was really good about coming back when he was called but because he was so big they had to be careful about letting him loose in case people were scared of him.

"I can't see anyone else… Yes, we'll let him off for the minute. It's more fun for him sniffing around in the bracken off the lead."

As Hugo ambled ahead, Lily and Dad chatted about what they were going to do over the summer. They'd gone on a brilliant holiday to a water park in half-term, so they weren't going away.

"I want to sort out the garden shed," Dad told Lily. "It's so full of junk, I can hardly get the lawnmower out."

"That's not very exciting!" Lily said, laughing. "You'll have to be careful though, Dad, have you seen the size of the spiders in that shed? I went in there yesterday to get the water guns and I'm sure I saw one the size of my hand."

"Mmm. I might wear gloves." Dad wrinkled his nose. "I suppose we should head back, it's almost time for lunch. Hugo! Come on, boy!"

Hugo was a little way away, gazing

curiously through the bracken, his tail wagging.

"Has he seen another dog?" Dad wondered, hurrying over. "Oh! Honestly. That's awful!"

"What is it?"

"Someone's dumped a load of stuff here, instead of taking it to the tip." Dad pointed to a pile of furniture – an old sofa and a fridge and what looked like some kitchen units. "What a mess! I'll have to ring the council when we get home, see if they'll come and take it away. I suppose the woods do back on to all those houses. Someone must have driven down the alleyway to the garages – yes, look, the fence is broken. It wouldn't have been too hard to get the stuff through here."

"That's really sad." Lily looked at the mess, frowning. "Hey, Hugo. Where are you going, silly? That's not a sofa for sitting on!" Hugo wasn't supposed to sit on any sofas but it was his one bad habit. He would lie at Dad's feet with his nose on the sofa, and gradually creep further and further forward until he could sneak his front paws on. He never got very far before he was pushed off – but he never gave up trying, either. He just wanted to be snuggled up with his family.

"Here, boy, come on," Dad called. "Hugo!"

But Hugo didn't come back like he usually did. He was sniffing at the old sofa, his plumy tail swishing really fast.

"Maybe it smells of food," Dad said, edging his way through the bracken to follow him. "It must smell of something, look at him, he's really excited. Hugo, leave it, come on!"

Hugo's ears were pricked right forward now, and he was whining and grunting and sniffing at the tatty sofa cushions.

Lily went after Dad, wriggling sideways through the undergrowth – she only had shorts on and there were nettles in among the bracken but she wanted to see what Hugo was so excited about.

Hugo had his nose down the back of the sofa cushions now. Then suddenly he jumped back with a snort.

"What is it?" Lily asked, leaning

over – and then she gasped.

Between the cushions and the back of the sofa was a squirming mass of fur. A litter of tiny, fluffy kittens!

Chapter Two

"Kittens!" Lily gasped. "Oh, wow! Did Hugo smell them? Or maybe he heard something?"

The kittens were squirming around, making tiny breathy squeaking noises. Hugo had moved the seat cushion with his nose while he was sniffing them out, so their cosy dark nest had been disturbed. Now the big dog was staring down at the kittens with his ears pricked right forward again. Dad had put a hand on his collar, just in case. After all, Hugo really didn't like Pixie, so it made sense that he wouldn't like the kittens, either. But right now he looked interested rather than grumpy.

Lily crouched down next to Hugo so she could look, too. There were three kittens – two tabbies and a gorgeous, little white kitten. Their fur looked quite long and fluffy to Lily, longer than Pixie's, she was sure. Perhaps they were going to be longhairs – like Persians. But they didn't have squashed Persian noses.

"I don't understand." Lily looked around. "Why would anyone put kittens down the back of a sofa? They should have taken them to an animal shelter, not just dumped them in the woods. It's a horrible thing to do!"

Dad nodded. "It is weird. Unless... Yes, that could be it. Maybe it was the mother cat."

"You mean, she had her babies out here in the woods?" Lily looked doubtful. Why would a cat want to have kittens in a grubby old sofa?"

"Cats do pick funny places sometimes. Grandma's cat had a litter of kittens in her wardrobe when she was a little girl, I remember her telling me."

"But why the woods instead of at home?" Lily looked up at Dad anxiously. "Maybe the mum doesn't have a home. Do you think she might be a stray?"

"Could be," Dad agreed. He glanced around, peering through the trees. "I wonder where she is. They look too small to be left alone for very long."

Just then the white kitten wriggled round and let out a squeaky little mew. Lily laughed delightedly. He – or she – was so cute, with a tiny pink nose and blue eyes. Even though his eyes were open, Lily didn't think he could really see her – his eyes didn't seem to be focusing. He was weaving his head about though, snuffing at the air. Lily wondered if he could smell Hugo.

Or perhaps he was just upset that their mum was gone and their nest had been disturbed.

"If their eyes are open, that means they've got to be a few days old, doesn't it?" Lily said, trying to think. She'd read somewhere that kittens were born with their eyes closed.

"Ye-ees." Dad nodded. "I guess so. But I'm still pretty sure they need their mum. They're too young to be walking around – they're just squirming about and wriggling on top of each other, aren't they?" He looked around again. "There's no sign of the mother cat. I wonder what it's best to do."

"Don't you think we should take them home, Dad?" Lily said pleadingly. "We can't leave them out here on their own, not when they're so little. They can't find any food for themselves, can they? Don't they still need their mum's milk?"

Dad shook his head. "Their mum could just have gone looking for food – she might be back any minute. Or maybe she actually *is* around here somewhere but she's too scared of us to come back to her kittens. I mean, no cat's going to walk up to Hugo…"

Hugo was still watching the kittens as though they were the best thing he'd seen in ages. He was following them with his nose as they clambered over and around each other, still squeaking.

"I think he likes them," Lily said, smiling. But then her smile faded. "What are we going to do, Dad? We can't just leave them and hope their mum comes back. What if she doesn't? They *need* her. Or somebody to look after them, anyway."

Dad frowned. "You know what? I'm going to ring the animal shelter where we got Hugo. I've got their number in my phone. I bet they'll know what to do."

Lily nodded. That was definitely a good idea. The staff at the shelter must have to deal with abandoned kittens all the time. She listened as her dad called up and explained about the kittens.

"No, we haven't seen the mum at all. Do you think she won't come back while we're here? No, I suppose not, if she's a stray… So, what do you think, should we leave them?"

"Oh no…" Lily whispered to herself, looking over at the tiny kittens. The little white one had ended up underneath the other two now. Lily longed to pick him up – surely it couldn't be good for him to be squashed like that?

She breathed a sigh of relief as he

wriggled out and accidentally nudged Hugo's nose with his own. Hugo stepped back, surprised, and Lily giggled.

"You like them, don't you?" Lily whispered to Hugo as he rested his chin on the arm of the sofa, gazing at the kittens.

Lily turned back to Dad. Surely the shelter couldn't be telling him to leave the kittens here? She couldn't bear to think of them all on their own.

"I'm really not sure how long she's been away, that's the thing," her dad was saying. "Amberdale Woods, that's right. Mmmm. Yes, we could do that. Will there be someone answering the phone later this evening? OK, I'll get back to you then. Thanks."

"What did they say?" Lily burst out.

"They think the mum's probably right here somewhere, hiding out and watching till we go away."

"Oh…" Lily looked around the woods, golden and silent in the sunlight. "But what if she's not? What if she doesn't come back?"

"Well, that's the problem. If she doesn't, I'm afraid the kittens won't last long without her. They're just too little to survive by themselves. They'll have to be taken to the shelter for hand-rearing – that means someone feeding them with a special bottle. So, we need to see what happens."

Dad made an apologetic face at Lily. "I said we'd keep an eye on them and watch out for their mum, Lils. It might be a bit boring. The lady from the shelter said we needed to give the mother cat a few hours before we do anything like moving the kittens."

"I don't mind! I don't want to leave them – even Hugo doesn't, look at him."

Dad nodded. "He's really fascinated,

isn't he? It's funny when you think how he is about Pixie. Maybe he doesn't understand that these are cats, too..." He smiled at Lily. "It's OK. I'm sure the mum will turn up soon if we get out of her way. Come on, Hugo," He looked around the clearing as Hugo paced slowly over to his side. "So now we need to find somewhere to watch from."

Lily stepped back reluctantly from the sofa and the kittens. The white kitten was on the top of the pile now, weaving his head from side to side. She longed to pick him up and cuddle him, and tell him everything was going to be OK but she knew she mustn't...

The white kitten mewed, calling miserably for his mother. He wanted milk – he kept blundering about, trying to suck but she wasn't there. He didn't understand. She had always been there to feed him before. She seemed to have been gone for so long and he was so hungry.

He hooked his tiny claws into the fabric at the back of the sofa and hauled himself up, sniffing the air, trying to find his mother. There was no warm, milky smell but he *could* smell something else, something different. He mewed uncertainly and sniffed the air again. The smell seemed to have moved away. Confused and worn out by the effort, he nuzzled into the furry pile of other kittens and settled back to sleep.

Chapter Three

"Lily, are you sure you don't want to go home?" Dad asked. "Mum just texted. She says she can walk up and get you and take Hugo back, too. We've been watching for an hour now. You must be getting hungry – it's past lunchtime."

Lily shook her head firmly. "I don't want to go home. And I don't mind not having any lunch."

They were sitting on a fallen tree with Hugo at their feet, just close enough to see the abandoned sofa through the bracken. Lily was pretty sure they were far enough away not to worry the mother cat, as long as they were quiet. The sofa wasn't that far from the main paths through the wood, so she must have been coming

and going with people and dogs around.

"Please, Dad," Lily begged, as Dad started to text Mum back. "I really want to stay and make sure the kittens are OK. I know we've been here an hour but that's a whole hour that their mum hasn't come back to look after them. That can't be right, can it? She's been gone ages."

Dad nodded. "It does seem a long time to me but I'm not really sure how often tiny kittens need to be fed. I don't think we can stay here all day, Lily. Perhaps we can keep popping back to check on them."

"But there's so many people who walk their dogs in this wood," Lily pointed out. "I know Hugo just wants to look at the kittens but another dog might hurt them."

They'd seen quite a few dog walkers already but luckily none of the dogs had come close enough to sniff out the kittens. Dad had asked the owners if they'd seen a cat around but they'd all said no. One lady had even offered to go home and ring the RSPCA when Dad and Lily told her about the kittens but Dad had explained they'd already called the shelter.

"OK," Dad said, putting his phone away. "I've told Mum we'll stay."

"What do you think could have happened to their mum?" Lily asked, a little while later. "I don't think she's coming back, Dad. Why would she leave them?"

Dad sighed. "I don't know. Perhaps she just couldn't look after them properly. The lady from the shelter did say that if a very young cat has kittens, they do sometimes abandon them. Because they just haven't got the energy to feed themselves and make enough milk for the kittens, too. If she's a stray and she's having to hunt for her food, or steal it out of bins, she might not be able to cope."

"That's so sad." Lily sighed, thinking of Pixie next door – so plump and well fed.

"Or it could be that she's not a stray. Maybe she just came here to have her kittens, and now her family have found her and they're keeping her in to stop her going off again."

"But they must know the kittens need her!" Lily shook her head. "Nobody would be that mean!"

Dad nodded. "No, you're probably right. I'm sure the owners would want to look after the kittens, too. Unless maybe they didn't realize she was pregnant…?"

Dad looked over towards the gap in the fence and the alleyway that led down to the houses and frowned. "Lily, listen, love. I don't want to upset you but there is another thing that could have happened. It's quite a busy road out there. She could have been hit by a car."

Lily swallowed and her voice wobbled when she answered. "I know. I was thinking that. We go down that road to school and cars do go really fast along there. Do you think she tried to cross it?"

"If she doesn't come back we'll probably never know." Dad put his arms round her shoulders. "But it's a possibility."

"Poor cat," Lily whispered. "And poor kittens."

"Well, at least we found them, thanks to Hugo."

"He's a hero." Lily rubbed his nose and Hugo turned to look back at her for a moment. Then his ears twitched and he stood up, gazing down the path.

"Someone's coming," Lily murmured. "Oh, it's Mum! And Carly! But I said I didn't want to go back, Dad."

"Hello!" Lily's mum stood on tiptoe, trying to see the sofa and the kittens. "We thought we'd come and bring you some sandwiches. Are they over there?"

"Can I go and see?" Carly asked.

"Just quickly," Dad suggested. "We're watching for their mum, Carly. We don't want to scare her off."

As Mum and Carly hurried over to take a quick look, Hugo stood up, whining a little.

"It's OK, boy." Dad patted him reassuringly. "He really is keeping watch over those kittens, isn't he?"

"They're beautiful," Mum whispered, as she and Carly came creeping back through the bracken. "But so tiny! Surely they're going to need feeding soon?"

Dad nodded. "I reckon so. But the lady at the shelter told us not to do anything until this evening. Just watch and wait."

"Lily, you're sure you don't want to come home with us? You've been out here for hours."

Lily shook her head. "Not yet, Mum, please. I'm so worried about them – and their mum," she added sadly. "Dad thinks she might have been run over."

"Oh, Lily." Mum hugged her.

"It's so lucky that Hugo sniffed them out," Lily murmured.

"I was going to say that we'd take him back," Mum said thoughtfully. "But looking at him, I'm not sure he'd come. He's had his eyes fixed on that sofa the whole time since we arrived.

Maybe he thinks that because he found the kittens he's got to look after them." She was smiling but she sounded half-serious.

Lily nodded. "German Shepherds are often guard dogs, aren't they? Hugo's guarding the kittens."

Chapter Four

Lily leaned forward eagerly, certain she'd seen a flash of white close by the old sofa. Perhaps the kittens' mum was a white cat – that would make sense. She started to say, "Dad…" but then she sighed. It wasn't the cat, after all. Just an old plastic bag, flapping in the breeze.

She shivered a little. Even though

it had been such a hot day, the woods were shady, especially now the sun was starting to go down. She peered over at the sofa, wondering if the kittens were feeling chilly, too. She and Dad had gone to check on them after Mum and Carly had left, and pulled the cushion back over them a little but she couldn't help worrying.

Over in the clearing, the white kitten huddled closer to his sisters, hunting for some warmth. Usually they were all snuggled up together against their mother but without her body heat the kittens were so small that they couldn't keep themselves warm. He was getting colder and colder, and it was getting hard to move. He squeaked for his mother again, calling to her to come back and feed them but she didn't come. Exhausted and hungry, the tiny kitten tried to crawl further under the cushions.

Lily shifted position again. She was getting pins and needles from sitting still for so long, and she was hungry. The sandwiches Mum had brought seemed a long time ago. She checked her watch. "Dad, it's six o'clock," she murmured, stretching out her feet and wriggling a bit.

"I know. I'm going to phone the shelter. It's been seven hours now." He took out his phone and Lily leaned closer to try to listen in.

"Hi, I rang earlier about some kittens our dog had found in Amberdale Woods. No, no sign of their mum coming back, I'm afraid. Would you be able to come and get them?"

He paused for a minute or so, listening, and Lily saw an anxious expression appear on his face – little creases over the top of his nose. "Oh… No, don't do that. Maybe we can help? Look, give me a minute. Let me talk to my wife and get back to you." He listened for a little longer, saying, "Mm-hm, mm-hm," and Lily squeezed even closer, desperate to know what was going on.

"Dad, what's happened?" she burst out, as soon as he ended the call.

"The shelter's really full. All of their foster carers have got kittens already. The manager was saying she'd ring round and see who could squeeze them in. Apparently this is kitten season." He laughed a little nervously.

"So what's going to happen to our kittens?" Lily asked. "Will they go to one of these foster people? Will they be all right?"

Dad was silent for a minute, running his hand down the back of Hugo's neck. "Actually, Lily, I'm wondering if we could take them. Just until they can find someone to foster them properly."

"What?" Lily squeaked. She was so surprised and excited she actually jumped up and down. "Do you mean it? We can take them home?"

"Hold on! Slow down a minute. I'm only talking about us looking after them until there's space for them with a foster carer. Since it's an emergency. And I said I'd have to talk to your mum about it. There's no point getting excited just yet."

"I know." Lily's voice was shaking. Those tiny kittens, hers to look after! If only Mum would say yes! She watched eagerly as Dad called home.

"Sarah, it's me. Yes, I called them but there's a problem – apparently they're really full. The lady I spoke to earlier on didn't realize but all their kitten fosterers have got litters of kittens. No, we're not going to leave them, listen! What do you think about us looking after them for a bit? The shelter manager – she's the one I just spoke to – said she'd send someone out to help us take them home. They'll bring some kitten formula and some information sheets on how to care for them if we agree."

He went quiet for a bit and Lily pressed closer. She could hear her mum's voice squeaking in the background and she wished Dad had put the speaker on.

"Yes, I know, the shelter manager mentioned that. I can't say I'm happy about getting up in the middle of the night but I feel responsible for them. They're so little—"

"Dad, what's the matter?" Lily interrupted. "What's Mum saying? Why can't we do it?"

"Because they're so young they'll need hand-rearing, Lily. Mum isn't sure we'll be up to it – we'd have to get up in the middle of the night, probably."

Lily grabbed his arm. "But I could help! Couldn't I? It's the summer holidays, I don't mind. Dad, please! It's like we were meant to find them – we came along just at the right time. We can't give up on them now!"

Dad sighed. "Did you hear all that?" he said into the phone. "Yes, I know. Maybe she is old enough to help out. You know how much she loves cats!"

"OK." Dad smiled at Lily. "Yes, I'll call the shelter back and tell them." He ended the call and laughed. "Wow. This was definitely not what I was expecting when we came out for a walk this morning."

"We'll put them in here," Amy explained, showing Lily and Dad a cardboard travel box that she'd brought with her. She seemed really nice, Lily thought. She'd told them she remembered Hugo from the shelter and that he'd grown into such a handsome, well-behaved dog.

"I've put a hot-water bottle in for them, wrapped up in some towels. If they've been without their mum all day, they'll be getting really cold. Kittens this young can't control their own temperature, you see. They need their mum's body heat to keep them warm. Even though it's been so hot today, if we leave them here overnight without her, they're at risk of hypothermia – that's getting too cold to survive."

"How old do you think they are?"

Lily asked, leaning over to look at the kittens. They were still moving – squirming around and nuzzling at each other – but she was sure they weren't as lively as they had been when they first saw them.

"Hard to say exactly. Maybe two to three weeks? Their eyes are open but they don't look big enough to be walking yet. Soon though."

"They don't look as bright as they did this morning," Dad said.

"I was thinking that, too." Lily bit her lip. "Oh no, maybe we waited for too long for their mum to come back."

Amy shook her head. "I don't think so. I know it sounds hard but the best person to look after them is definitely their mum – she's built for feeding them, cleaning them, keeping them warm. If we take them away from her, we're giving the kittens second-best. Do you see what I mean? So if there'd been any chance that their mum was going to come back and care for them, it was better to let her."

"Dad thinks she might have been run over," Lily said, gazing down at the kittens.

Amy nodded. "It's possible, I'm afraid. Or she may just not have been able to feed them. Either way, I think we have to assume she's not coming back."

She opened the travel box and gently reached in to pick up one of the tabby kittens. Hugo whined and Amy laughed. "You're such a good boy, aren't you? Are you taking over from their mum, Hugo?"

She put the kitten gently into the box and Hugo nosed at the cardboard flaps, clearly making sure that the kitten was all right. "We wouldn't usually put foster kittens with a family who had a dog but this is a bit of an emergency. Now, I'll come back to the house with you, if that's OK, and help you set up a safe pen to keep them in."

Amy picked up the other tabby kitten and Lily watched anxiously as the white kitten gave a feeble mew. The kitten looked so little, left all on his own. "Can I pick this one up?" Lily whispered. He was hardly moving.

"Sure."

Lily picked up the tiny kitten – he wasn't much bigger than her cupped hands – and carefully moved him over to the box. He squirmed around and gave another squeaky breath of a mew but then he cuddled up next to the two tabby kittens again, snuggling against the warmth of the hot-water bottle.

Lily looked up at Dad with shining eyes. "Let's take them home."

Chapter Five

Amy came back to the house to help settle the kittens in. She brought in a big box of equipment from her car – special kitten formula milk and kitten bottles and a litter tray. She explained that the kittens would need feeding about every four hours. "It's a lot of work," she said, looking round at them all. "Are you really sure you can manage?"

Mum was reading the instruction sheets, looking rather anxious. "Oh my goodness, I hadn't even thought about sterilizing," she murmured. "But I suppose it's just like feeding a baby. Have we still got the old sterilizer in the loft?"

Dad grinned. "Yes. Now aren't you grateful that I never sorted all that stuff out to go to the charity shop? I'll go and get it. We need to give them a feed as soon as possible, don't we?"

"Yes, that would be great." Amy looked pleased. "Having a sterilizer will definitely make things easier. Oh!" Amy turned round from the table. Hugo had nudged open the kitchen door and marched in, looking determined.

"Sorry, I'll take him out again."

Mum shook her head. "No, Hugo. You need to stay away from the kittens. It's going to be tricky keeping him out, he's used to having his basket and his food bowls in here."

"Wait a minute," Dad murmured. "Look at him. He's not at all bothered that they're in his kitchen. Even though we've moved his basket away from the radiator and put the box there instead."

Amy nodded. "I think you're right. And I was going to say that I'd try and get hold of a special heating pad for you, to keep the kittens warm but I'm not sure you're going to need it."

The kittens were still in their cardboard box, curled up on the hot-water bottle but now Hugo lay down and curled himself around it, so that they had his warmth, too. The kittens were already pressing up against the side of the box next to him. Even though they were so tiny, their instincts were telling them to warm up.

"Hugo really loves them." Lily smiled. She'd never have expected that Hugo would make a brilliant kitten nurse.

"Right," Amy continued. "I'll show you how to mix the milk powder and feed the kittens. And then – well, for another week or so, until they're old enough to do it themselves, I'm afraid you're going to have to help them wee and poo afterwards."

"That's disgusting!" Carly said, making a horrified face.

Amy laughed. "I know it sounds weird. But mother cats lick their kittens after they've fed them and that tells their bodies to wee or poo, you see. When you're hand-rearing kittens, you have to do everything their mum does. But with cotton wool, dampened with warm boiled water," she added hurriedly.

"Thank goodness for that," Dad murmured.

The white kitten woke up and looked around the dark room. He still couldn't see or smell his mother but at least he was properly warm. He remembered being fed, too, but now he was feeling hungry again. He staggered up on to his paws and mewed, calling for his mother. But instead of a fluffy tabby face, a large white nose came over the side of his box and nuzzled at him.

The kitten sniffed and then sneezed and looked up at the huge creature in confusion. This was most definitely not his mother. Whoever it was felt warm, though, and comforting. The kitten mewed again, asking the big dog for food, and felt his two tabby sisters stirring beside him. They started to call for milk, too.

"Hello, Hugo… Did they wake you up?" a deep voice said, laughing a little.

The kitten moved his head towards the sound and then let out a tiny squeak. Hugo had leaned down again, and picked him up – just the way his mother did – in his jaws. The kitten wriggled as he was lifted from the box but then he found himself between the dog's great paws, cosily nestled against the thick fur of his chest. Forgetting to be hungry for a moment, the kitten snuggled closer and drifted back to sleep.

Upstairs, Lily lay half awake. She'd been dreaming about the kittens and now she couldn't tell whether she was asleep or not. She could hear mewing – pitiful little squeaks – and low voices coming from downstairs. Of course! The night-time feed!

Mum and Dad had worked out that it would be best to feed the kittens at about eleven o'clock before they went to bed, then at three in the morning and then again when they all got up. Dad had said it would only be for a week or so, until the kittens were a bit older and could go for more than four hours without food.

Lily had begged to be allowed to

help but Mum and Dad had said it was far too late for her and Carly, even though it was the holidays.

But if they were feeding the kittens, why could she hear mewing? The little squeaks sounded desperate. Lily sat up worriedly. She had to make sure they were OK – especially the fluffy white one. He had felt so tiny in her hands when she lifted him into the box, as though there was hardly anything of him under all that fur.

Lily got out of bed, pulled on her dressing gown and fumbled sleepily for her slippers. Then she crept down the stairs.

She tiptoed along the hallway and peered into the kitchen. Her mum and dad were sitting at the table in their pyjamas, each with a tabby kitten in their laps. The kittens were busily sucking from the bottles.

"Lily! You should be asleep!" Dad sighed.

"I could hear mewing, it woke me up. What's wrong?"

"It's a bit tricky feeding more than one at once – the white kitten was asleep, so we thought we'd leave him till last but now he's woken up and he's not happy about waiting," Mum explained. "I expect he can smell the milk."

Lily was just about to crouch down and peer into the box when Hugo gave a mournful "Arrrooo!" and she realized that he had the kitten between his paws.

"Oh, Hugo's looking after him!"

"He lifted the kitten out of the box in his mouth," Dad told her. "I was a bit worried. But then I think mother cats do the same thing."

"Is all that mewing bothering you, Hugo?" Lily asked. Then she turned back to look at Mum and Dad. "Shall I feed him? Since I'm awake anyway? We've got another bottle and Hugo's getting upset, you can tell. He doesn't like Stanley crying like that."

"Stanley?" Mum smiled at her. "Since when is he called Stanley?"

Lily went pink. "I just think he looks like a Stanley. It's such a cute name."

"It is cute," Mum agreed, passing Lily a bottle. "But just remember we're not going to have them for long, Lily. Only until the shelter can find a foster home."

"I know." Lily gently scooped up the white kitten and carried him over to the table. Hugo followed her, resting his muzzle on her lap so he could watch what she was doing. Stanley seemed to have learned exactly what to do with the bottle from his two previous feeds – he practically jumped at it, sucking greedily at the milk with funny little slurping noises.

"Wow, you really were hungry," Lily murmured. "Mum, look, I think I can actually see his tummy getting bigger!"

Her mum laughed. "They're really guzzling it down, aren't they. Oh, Lily, listen!"

"I can feel it…" Lily whispered back. Stanley was purring.

Chapter Six

"Which one's your favourite?" Mara leaned over the kitten pen, admiring the three kittens. Lily had emailed her best friend to tell her about their amazing discovery, and Mara had been desperate to come and see the kittens as soon as she'd got back from her holiday in Spain.

They were about five weeks old

now – big enough to walk around really well. They stomped all over each other, squeaking loudly, and they were always wrestling and jumping out at each other. They loved playing with all the toys Lily had persuaded Mum and Dad to get from the pet shop, too. Their favourite was a feathery stick, a bit like a feather duster, and Lily spent ages waving it about for them.

Dad had found a big shallow plastic storage box up in the loft when he was looking for the sterilizer and he'd brought it down to use as a pen to keep the kittens in. It meant they had space to move around but they were safer than they would be loose in the kitchen. But it hadn't lasted long. They still used it to sleep in but they'd learned to wriggle and scramble their way out after just a few days.

"Stanley – he's my favourite," Lily said, pointing him out. "He's like a little fluffy snowball!"

"He is cute," Mara agreed. "But I love the stripes on the other two as well. Isn't it loads of work looking after them all?"

"They're starting to eat proper food now – special kitten food mixed with a bit of their milk. At least that means we can just feed them really late at night and then early in the morning. No one has to get up in the middle of the night any more." Lily reached her hand into the plastic box and Stanley staggered determinedly towards her, licking at her fingers.

“They’re so gorgeous. If it was me, I don’t think I’d be able to give them away,” Mara said, lifting one of the tabby kittens on to her lap. They were both girls, and Carly had named them Bella and Trixie. “You’ve spent your whole summer holiday looking after them but then you don’t get to keep them. That doesn’t seem fair!”

"I know." Lily sighed. "But we were never going to keep them. They were originally supposed to go to another foster family as soon as they had the space. But when Amy came to check up on them, a couple of days after they came here, she said we were doing so well maybe we should just keep them until they were ready for rehoming. And luckily Mum and Dad said yes!" She smiled as Stanley butted his head against her hand and let out a squeaky little mew. "It's not food time yet, baby…"

"So they won't go to the shelter, then?"

"Their photos are up on the shelter website already but they'll just send anyone who's interested in adopting them round to us. So at least the kittens won't have to get used to a new place."

Mara nodded. "And I suppose you'll be able to see if the people are nice."

Lily nodded. She didn't like thinking about the kittens' new owners – especially not Stanley's. Even though she was making the best of it to Mara, she couldn't imagine not having a box of kittens in their kitchen... But they already had Hugo.

"Do you think Hugo will miss them?" Mara asked, as she heard scrabbling at the kitchen door.

Lily opened the door, checking that the kittens weren't about to dart through and Hugo trotted in, immediately coming over to inspect his kittens.

"Definitely." Lily stroked his nose. "He does that every time he's been out for a walk. He has to come back and make sure they're all OK. Yes, don't worry, I looked after them for you. Trixie's over there, see?"

Hugo was looking around for the other tabby kitten, and when he spotted her peeking out from behind the kitchen bin he went to round her up, gently nosing her back over towards the plastic box.

"He wants them all in the box the whole time," Lily explained. "He's like a sheepdog, herding them about." She watched proudly as Hugo picked up the tabby kitten in his mouth and dropped her, wriggling, back into the box.

"I thought he was biting her!" Mara said, looking a bit worried.

"No. He's so gentle. He just holds them in his mouth. Their mum would have done the same thing. Oh, Hugo, look, Stanley's coming out now."

The white kitten was clambering out of the box, half falling, half jumping out on to the kitchen tiles. Hugo seemed almost to sigh. He lay down in front of the box between the two girls, making a big furry barrier between Stanley and the rest of the kitchen.

Stanley nuzzled him, nose to nose, and both girls "aaahhed". Stanley marched along the whole length of Hugo and started to pat at his feathery tail as Hugo twitched it from side to side and then jumped on it with fierce little growls. Hugo watched him, clearly enjoying the game. As soon as Stanley was clinging on with all four paws, he swished his tail faster so that the kitten swept across the floor and both girls burst out laughing.

"They go together so well," Mara said. "Both of them white and fluffy."

"I know." Lily nodded. They really did. If only they could keep Stanley, he and Hugo would be a perfect pair.

Lily giggled as Stanley wobbled down her bed. He wasn't very good at walking on the squishy duvet and he kept nearly falling over. He stopped to inspect her teddy bear and then jumped at it, sinking his tiny claws into the ribbon around its neck.

Lily was so busy watching Stanley, she didn't notice the gentle scuffling noises from outside her bedroom window. Then there was a loud hiss and she glanced round in surprise. Pixie was standing on the sloping roof, peering in at the open window, the fur on the back of her neck raised. She was clearly furious – this was her place and now there was another cat.

"Oh, Pixie, no!" Lily stared at her anxiously. What was she going to think of Stanley? She'd been in Lily's room a couple of times since they'd got the kittens but Lily had quickly shut her door so Pixie didn't go downstairs. This was the first time Pixie had seen one of them.

Lily dithered, not sure whether to grab Stanley or try to shoo Pixie out. She didn't want to push her back through the window, in case she slipped. Pixie came further in, climbing on to Lily's windowsill and hissing loudly, her tail fluffing up.

"No!" Lily said sharply, seeing Stanley cower back against the teddy bear, his own fur starting to stand up, too. "Pixie, out! This isn't your house!"

She sat up, trying to grab Pixie. Perhaps she could take her downstairs and put her out of the front door. "I know you've been in here before, I'm sorry, Pixie. Ow!" Pixie had swiped her paw down Lily's arm, leaving two bright red scratches. Then she hissed again, spat angrily at Stanley and darted back out of the window.

Lily shut the window, rather shakily. Pixie had never scratched her before. Then she glanced round at Stanley.

He was huddled into a tiny white ball on her bed and he looked terrified.

"Oh, Stanley, I'm sorry, sweetheart. It's OK. She's not coming back in."

Gently, Lily lifted him up in her cupped hands and snuggled him up against her T-shirt.

"It's all right, I'll look after you, shh. I wish I could just look after you always," she added sadly. The shelter had called Mum that morning to say a lady had seen the kittens on their website and wanted to come and visit them. She was interested in the two tabbies but Lily knew it wouldn't be long until someone wanted to take Stanley, too.

Stanley huddled against her, his heart thumping. He didn't understand what had just happened. He had been enjoying playing with Lily by himself, without his sisters climbing all over her, too. He loved it when she fussed over him and played with him and then let him snooze on her lap when he was tired out. But suddenly the other cat had appeared, one that Stanley had never seen before.

Hugo nosed his way round Lily's door and padded across the room.

"Did you hear Pixie?" Lily murmured. "She was really cross. Oh, you can smell her, can't you?"

Hugo's ears had flattened back and he was sniffing at Lily's bed. Then he nudged Stanley gently. The white kitten rubbed his head against the huge dog's muzzle and then stepped back with a squeak as Hugo licked him, his big pink tongue practically covering the tiny kitten.

"Hugo!" Lily giggled. "Look at him, you've flattened his fur!"

"They're so beautiful… I wish we could take all of them but I think three cats might be too many." Candace smiled at Lily and Carly and their mum. "You've done so well, hand-rearing them. They're so big and healthy-looking. You did an amazing job!"

Mum put her arm round Lily's shoulders. "To be honest, it was mostly Lily. She's worked really hard – she even did some of the night feeds. I can't believe how big they are now. Seven weeks old! The time's gone so fast."

Far too fast, Lily thought to herself.

"I suppose if they were still with their mum, it would be too early for us to adopt them," Candace said thoughtfully. "It's very lucky for us, getting to have such small kittens. We're really grateful. Aren't we, Jack?"

Her little boy nodded. He had Bella on his lap and he was running one finger carefully down her back all the way from the top of her head to her tail, over and over. Bella was nuzzling his hand, purring, and Jack looked as though his dream had come true.

Even though Lily hated the thought of someone else taking her lovely kittens home, she could see that Candace and Jack were going to be amazing cat owners. At least they were only taking Bella and Trixie, she thought sadly. She wondered how Stanley would feel all on his own.

Stanley watched, confused, as the strange people put his sisters into a cat carrier. They were mewing, not sure what was happening, and he squeaked back anxiously. Where were they going? And why wasn't he going, too?

He hurried to the edge of the plastic box as the kitchen door opened and they all started to walk out – those people were taking his sisters away! Panicking, he clawed his way up the side of the box, his paws slipping, and scrambled out on to the floor to chase after them. But the door closed before he was halfway there, and he sat under the table and mewed frantically.

He jumped up when the door opened again and Lily let Hugo in. The big dog came nosing under the table and lowered his head to Stanley. He licked the kitten with one great swipe of his huge pink tongue and then slumped down to the floor next to him, resting his muzzle between his paws.

Stanley patted at one of Hugo's long white paws, nibbled it and then snuggled wearily into the kitten-sized space between Hugo's paw and his nose, curling up into a sad little ball.

Chapter Seven

"Night, Mum." Lily peered round her mum's office door on her way to bed. "Oh, that one's so cute. Wow, you can really see how fluffy he's getting." Lily leaned over her mum's shoulder, admiring the photos of Stanley on her computer. "What are you looking at the photos for? Are you sending them to Grandma?" Lily's grandma loved cats, too. She lived in Scotland so she hadn't seen the kittens yet but Lily had been telling her all about them on the phone. Grandma had told Lily how jealous she was.

Her mum looked up. "No, I wasn't. Maybe I should though, I hadn't thought of that. I was actually looking for a good photo to send to Amy for the shelter website. The one they've got up there now is all the kittens together – we need one of just Stanley on his own."

Lily took a step back, suddenly feeling breathless. She knew that Stanley was going to be adopted, too, of course she did. But this made it all too real – and too soon. He looked so cute in the photo on Mum's screen –

he had his mouth open in a mew and his little pink tongue was showing. His eyes were shining emerald green and his fur was standing out around his head in a fluffy halo. Anybody would want to adopt him, Lily thought miserably. Who could resist such a gorgeous boy?

"Oh, Lily..." Mum turned round in her chair, reaching out to hug her. "I know you love him..."

"Couldn't we keep him?" Lily pleaded. "He's so special..." Her voice wobbled and her throat felt like it was closing up. She couldn't get any more words out.

"You know we were only looking after them for a little while, darling."

Lily nodded and sniffed and then dashed out of Mum's office, racing upstairs to her bedroom. She flung herself down on her bed, burying her face in her pillow, her eyes full of tears. Why couldn't they keep Stanley? He got on amazingly with Hugo. Mara had been right when she said they made a perfect pair. Hugo had looked after Stanley all morning after Bella and Trixie had gone. In fact, Lily was pretty sure that Hugo would be as upset as her if Stanley went to a new home.

She just had to explain all that properly to Mum and Dad. Lily rubbed her eyes and sniffed determinedly. Maybe she should write down a list of reasons to keep Stanley, just to make sure she didn't forget any of them. And then she would find just the right time to convince her family…

Lily woke up suddenly, her heart racing. She sat up in bed and peered around anxiously, trying to work out what was wrong. Everything in her room looked strange and ghostly in the darkness. Why had she jumped awake like that?

She was just about to settle down again, fussing with the crumpled sheet and wishing the night wasn't so hot, when loud barking erupted downstairs – mixed with ear-splitting yowls. Hugo was obviously furious, it was his angry bark, over and over again – and then there was a crashing sound.

Lily flung back the sheet and headed downstairs at a run, not even stopping to think what was going on. Something awful was happening. She could hear voices in Mum and Dad's room – they'd clearly been woken up, too, and Carly appeared in her bedroom doorway as Lily started down the stairs.

She was surprised to see the kitchen door was open but then realized that

Mum and Dad must have left it ajar to keep the room a bit cooler for Hugo and Stanley to sleep in. Hugo wouldn't come out of the kitchen anyway, he loved his basket. But maybe Stanley had come out of the kitchen and got lost in the dark. Had that crash been him knocking something over in the living room, maybe? That wouldn't make Hugo react so badly though, would it? He was still barking – quieter barks now and furious growls. Lily couldn't remember ever hearing him so upset.

Lily switched on the kitchen light, murmuring, "Stanley? Hugo? What's the matter?" Then she gasped. The kitchen looked as though someone had run round pushing everything that they could find off the surfaces. The pile of newspapers from the recycling box was scattered all over the place. The vase of flowers that had been in the middle of the kitchen table was tipped over, cascading water down on to the tiles. There was even a mug smashed on the floor just below the sink.

Hugo was standing in front of the sink, growling angrily at the window above it. Lily shivered, suddenly wondering if there had been someone in the garden? Perhaps Hugo had been woken by a burglar? Could he have made all this mess just by jumping about, trying to raise the alarm? Even though he wasn't usually clumsy, he did sometimes knock things over by flailing his tail around when he was really excited.

"It's OK, Hugo, shh," Lily murmured. "What's wrong? And where's Stanley?" she added. When she'd gone to bed, Stanley had been curled up in Hugo's basket, snuggled in between Hugo's paws, and both of them had been asleep. There was no little white kitten in the dog basket now, or in the big plastic box.

"Stanley?" Lily called worriedly. Where was he? She ducked down, searching under the table and behind the bin but there was no little white kitten.

"Lily, what's going on?" Dad hurried into the kitchen, with Mum and Carly close behind. "Wow! What happened here?"

"I don't know! Hugo's really upset and I can't find Stanley. He isn't anywhere."

Hugo came over to Dad, sniffing and nosing at his hands, and Dad rubbed his ears comfortingly. "Hey, he's got a scratch on his nose," Dad said. "What happened, boy?"

"Oh, Hugo, did you cut yourself on that broken mug?" Mum crouched down to look, too.

Hugo pulled away and padded over to the sink cabinet again, this time leaping up and planting his paws on the edge of the sink. He wasn't supposed to jump up like that but nobody stopped him.

Then a little white face peered out from behind the curtains. Stanley – with his long white fur all fluffed up. He was huddling in the corner of the windowsill, looking terrified.

"There he is!" Lily exclaimed gratefully. "How on earth did you get up there?" She hurried over to the windowsill, picking up Stanley and cuddling him close. She'd never have thought that Stanley could make the jump on to the counter – he must have jumped on to a chair to get him halfway. "Come on, Stanley, it's OK. What happened?"

"It's pretty obvious," Dad said anxiously. "They've been fighting. Hugo couldn't have cut his nose on that mug, not unless it actually fell on him. That's a cat scratch."

Lily could feel the white kitten's heart hammering and his ears were laid back. Hugo dropped back down to the floor and stood looking up at

Stanley in Lily's arms.

"That can't be right," Lily said, shaking her head. "Stanley loves Hugo. They were even asleep together in Hugo's basket when I went to bed! And Hugo wouldn't hurt Stanley."

"He didn't!" Carly said angrily, crouching down beside Hugo and putting her arm round him. "Stanley hurt *him*! Look at his poor nose!"

Mum sighed. "We don't know which of them started it. I suppose we've been lucky we haven't had any issues with them until now – it's weird this has happened so suddenly... But if they're going to start fighting with each other, we'll have to talk to Amy in the morning. Stanley's old enough to stay at the shelter now until they find a home for him. Hopefully they've got room."

"What?" Lily gasped. "No, Mum, he's staying here. We said we'd look after him until we found him a proper home. He can't go to the shelter!"

"He has to, Lily," Dad said gently. "I know you've loved having the kittens here and you've worked so hard with them but we can't risk Stanley being hurt if he and Hugo aren't getting on. What if Stanley tries to scratch Hugo again and Hugo lashes out? I know Hugo wouldn't deliberately hurt him – at least, I don't think he would – but he's just so much bigger than Stanley. It's not safe."

"And this is Hugo's home!" Carly put in.

"She's right, Lily," Dad said. "We can't send Hugo away."

Lily shook her head, tears starting to well up in her eyes. Stanley wriggled a little as one fell on to his nose and he licked it, liking the salty taste.

This couldn't be happening, Lily thought, looking miserably from Dad to Mum to Carly. Everyone seemed to be certain that Stanley had to go. How could this be happening now? Tomorrow was supposed to be the start of her grand plan to convince everyone they could keep their gorgeous kitten forever – and now instead he was going to be sent to the shelter.

"He just can't," she whispered. "He'll hate it there. We saw the cats when we went to get Hugo – they had those little rooms. He's used to a whole big kitchen and my bedroom. He'll be so lonely without us." *And without Hugo*, Lily added in her head. She still couldn't understand what had happened. Hugo had never barked at the kittens – not even when he'd first found them in the woods. He'd looked after them so carefully – Stanley even slept in his basket. This just wasn't right.

But nobody was listening to her. It felt like all the plans were already made – Mum and Dad were discussing who could go and drop off Stanley at the shelter. Carly was still petting Hugo and glaring at the kitten.

"What are we going to do with them tonight?" Dad murmured, looking between Stanley and Hugo. "We can't leave them both in here, obviously."

"I'll take Stanley upstairs with me," Lily said quickly. It was their last night, she realized. Her last time to cuddle him. "I'll take his box upstairs with me and put it by my bed."

Mum nodded. "OK. But shut your door, Lily."

"I'll bring the box for you," Dad said. He picked it up and followed her up the stairs.

Lily couldn't help crying into Stanley's fur as she took him up to her room. He was still so little – far too little to go to the shelter, she was sure. It would be like sending him off for his first day of school. She half laughed, half sniffed at the thought.

"I'm really going to miss this one," Dad said, rubbing one finger under Stanley's chin as Lily climbed into bed, still holding him. She put him down gently on top of the sheet and Stanley started to wander around the folds, his paws sliding.

"Oh, Lily, don't cry, sweetheart." Dad put his arm round her. "He'll go to a lovely new home. He's so gorgeous, he probably won't even be in the shelter for a day."

"I don't want him to have a lovely new home," Lily sobbed. "I want him to stay here!"

"I know." Dad sighed. "I had been thinking that, too… But this is Hugo's home, Lily, love. You know that."

"I still can't believe they were fighting…" Lily whispered.

Stanley came stomping back up the bed towards her and began to clamber on to her legs, wriggling as he got caught up in the sheet. Dad laughed and helped him up with a hand under his bottom. "There you go, Stanley. Night, Lily." He went over to close the bedroom window. "Just in case – we don't want Stanley getting out. I hope it's not too hot. Everything will be OK, honestly."

Lily watched him go, blowing her a kiss from the doorway and then closing the door behind him. *How can everything possibly be OK?* she thought sleepily, as Stanley padded round and round on her tummy, making himself a comfy little nest. *It's not OK at all*...

Stanley tucked his nose under his tail and closed his eyes. He loved the feeling of snuggling up on top of Lily. He could tell that there was something wrong, her breathing sounded different, with strange little hitches that made him bounce on her tummy each time. But he'd never been able to sleep on her bed before – it was even better than curling up next to Hugo. He was warm and safe...

His ears flattened back for a moment

as he suddenly remembered and he let out a little mew of fright. He'd been fast asleep and then the barking had woken him. Stanley had never heard Hugo bark like that before – he was protecting his house. He'd been trying to protect Stanley, too, but the noise was still so scary.

Stanley had run madly around the kitchen, trying to find a hiding place but nowhere had felt safe. In the end he'd jumped on to the kitchen table and then made a flying leap on to the counter, scrabbling madly and nearly falling back down. He'd huddled himself behind the curtains, curling up as small as he could as the barking and hissing went on and on.

Stanley stood up, pacing round and

round on the bed to calm himself down. Lily shifted a little, with a wheezy moan, and settled again. Then, at last, they slept.

Chapter Eight

"Do you think they'll want his toys at the shelter?" Mum said doubtfully, holding up a catnip mouse with half its tail gone and a hole where the stuffing was coming out.

"He loves that mouse," Lily said, with a catch in her voice. "You have to take it!" She abandoned her cereal – she wasn't hungry anyway – and got down on the kitchen floor, looking for all the jingly balls, feathers and other toys that were scattered about. Of course, Stanley's favourite toy was Hugo, she realized, looking at them both under the table. Mum and Dad had decided that as long as someone stayed with them both the whole time, it was OK to let them be in the same room until Mum took Stanley to the shelter.

Hugo was lying full length under the table – probably hoping for Carly's toast crusts – and Stanley was playing with his paws. He was hopping over them, pouncing and patting at them with his own. Every so often Hugo would yawn and move a paw a little, so that Stanley leaped on it with ferocious tigerish growls.

Mum kept turning round from the bacon she was cooking and glancing over at them, obviously checking that they weren't about to fight again but they weren't. It was a game, it always was. Lily stared at them, trying not to let herself start crying again. She still couldn't quite believe that this was happening. How could they be happy together now, when Hugo had been so furious last night and Stanley so terrified?

"Can you get that, Lily?" Mum said, as the doorbell rang. "I don't want to leave this pan. It's probably just the post."

Lily got up and went to the door, opening it just as her dad came downstairs. Their next-door neighbour,

Anna, was standing there, looking worried.

"Hi, Anna." Dad came over to the door. "Is everything all right?"

Anna smiled. "I hope so... But I've come to apologize, just in case."

"OK..." Dad said, looking puzzled. "Would you like some coffee? We're just having breakfast."

"Oh, I didn't mean to interrupt!"

"Honestly, it's fine."

"I'd love a coffee." Anna smiled, and followed Lily and Dad through to the kitchen, where Mum was dishing out the bacon.

"I do feel bad, though," Anna continued. "I've a horrible feeling that Pixie's been in here again. She bolted in through the cat flap at about midnight, in a bit of a state. She was soaking wet and all the fur that wasn't plastered down with water was sticking up. And I heard a lot of barking, so I wondered if she'd climbed through Lily's window again and had had a bit of a bust-up with Hugo… You mentioned she'd come in that way before."

Anna looked between Mum and Dad as the whole family stared at her. "I really am sorry," she added. "I know she's a nightmare. My neighbours on the other side got quite cross with her the other day – they found her on the kitchen table licking the butter…" Her voice trailed away. "Oh no, what did she do?"

"It was Pixie!" Lily breathed, remembering her open bedroom window. "It was Pixie, not Stanley! Hugo was barking at Pixie!" And that meant Stanley didn't need to go…

"Mum, do you think…?" Lily put her hand on Mum's arm, trying to get her to listen, but Mum was looking at Anna and not paying attention.

"She was in here, then. Oh dear..." Anna looked around the kitchen. "I really hope she didn't break anything."

Dad laughed. "Actually, I think she broke a mug but don't worry, Anna. That's about the best news you could have given us. We came down last night because Hugo was barking his head off to find the kitchen in a bit of a mess and Hugo with a scratch on his nose. No, no, it's OK!" he added, seeing Anna put a hand up to her mouth. "You see, we thought it was Stanley who'd done it. We were going to take him to the animal shelter this morning and now we don't have to!"

"Pixie scratched Hugo?" Anna looked down at Hugo guiltily. "Poor Hugo. She's a horror, she really is."

"But you love her to bits," Mum said, laughing.

"I'd better start locking the cat flap at night." Anna sighed.

"Mum." Lily pulled at her sleeve. "Mum, listen, please, it's important. You need to call the shelter."

Mum gave her a hug. "It's OK, Lily, you don't need to tell me. We'll call them right now and let them know we don't need to bring Stanley in after all."

"I should have listened when you said that Hugo wouldn't have been barking like that at Stanley," Dad said, shaking his head. "I mean just look at them."

Everyone looked down under the table. Stanley, worn out from his game, was collapsed over Hugo's enormous paws. As they stared at him, he opened one eye lazily, just a slit of green peering up at them all.

"Please…" Lily whispered. "Couldn't we keep him? I know we had Hugo first but Hugo loves him, too."

"Can we?" Carly put in. "It would make Hugo sad if he had to go," she admitted. "I think Stanley should stay."

"Yes! Oh, Carly, thank you!" Lily hugged her sister tight.

Mum smiled. "I'd better go and ring the shelter, hadn't I?"

"What are you going to say to them?" Lily asked anxiously.

"I'm going to ask them to take his photo off the website – he's already got a home."

Lily threw her arms round her mum and then her dad and even Anna – she wanted to hug everyone. Then she crouched down beside Stanley and Hugo. "You're staying," she said, stroking the fluffy white fur on Stanley's tummy. You're our kitten now!"

Stanley opened the other eye and stretched, rolling over on to his back and padding his front paws against Hugo's nose. Hugo snorted, shifted his head and gently licked the little kitten.

Stanley uncurled himself from the big dog and stood up, stretching again and arching his back as he yawned. He padded deliberately over to Lily, and rubbed the side of his head lovingly up and down her shorts. He climbed on to her knees and stood up, nudging her chin with the top of his head and purring loudly. Then he jumped down and touched noses with Hugo.

"They're perfect," Lily whispered, crouching down to stroke Hugo. "They belong together, here with us."

Read an extract from the latest kitten adventure

Chapter One

Amina raced up the steps at the front of the animal shelter and twirled round and round in front of the door. "Come on!" she called to the rest of the family. "Zara! Hurry up! Don't you want to see the kittens?"

Zara didn't dash after her twin sister. She pushed her hand into Dad's instead, holding on to him tight. She wanted to go and meet the kittens, of course she did. It was just that she was excited in a different way. She didn't do dancing about like Amina did. Her excitement was all inside, but it was definitely there. She and Amina had been talking about this moment for so long – imagining meeting their very own kitten for the first time.

Zara slipped the hand that wasn't holding Dad's into her pocket, closing it around the folded printout that she'd been carrying about for days, ever since Mum had emailed the animal shelter to say they were interested in the kittens. Zara had got her to print one of the photos, so she could keep looking at it. It showed all three kittens snuggled up in a soft cat bed, two tabby ones mostly on top of a little black-and-white one. She didn't seem to mind though. She looked quite comfy with a warm blanket of kitten on top of her.

"Excited?" Mum leaned over to look at Zara, smiling. "I know how much you've been looking forward to this."

Zara nodded hard and smiled back, but she still didn't say anything.

Up at the top of the steps, Amina was tugging open the heavy glass door…

When Mum and Dad had told the girls they would be able to go and see the kittens and choose which one they wanted to adopt, Zara had thought they'd only be allowed to look at them, maybe through a door into their pen. But instead they were taken to a special meeting room and James, the man who worked at the shelter, explained to them that they just needed to wait while he went to fetch the kittens.

"Do you think we'll get to hold them?" Zara asked Mum hopefully as James hurried off.

Amina nodded. "Look! There are cat toys in that basket. I think we can play with the kittens."

Zara looked round and saw a basket full of all different sorts of toys – balls, feathery birds, squishy mice… Just the kind of things she'd been thinking of buying with her pocket money, ever since Mum and Dad had said they could get a kitten when they'd moved to their new house.

Zara and Amina's mum had recently changed jobs. She now worked at a hospital that was too far away for her to commute. It was a huge change for everyone – Amina and Zara would have to start at a different school too. But there were some good things about moving. Mum and Dad had always said their old house was too small for pets, and it was by a busy road. The new house had a garden and it was really quiet. Perfect for a cat. Amina and Zara were going to be ten soon – ten was definitely old enough to look after a pet, and they'd promised to help lots. Mum and Dad had promised they would contact the animal shelter as soon as they'd settled in. Even though it had only been a couple of weeks, it felt like a very long wait…

"Is he coming back yet?" Amina asked, bouncing up from her chair.

"It won't be long," Mum said, laughing at her.

Dad turned to the door. "I think I can hear them, actually."

The girls stared hopefully at the

door – and Dad was right. James eased it open and stepped through with a cat carrier. Tiny, squeaky, cross little mews echoed from inside, until James set the carrier down and opened the wire door, and then there was a curious silence. Amina and Zara exchanged a wide-eyed look and Amina slipped her hand into Zara's. After all the waiting…

Two small tabby faces appeared at the door of the carrier and Zara caught her breath. Even Amina was too excited to speak – or perhaps she'd realized she needed to be quiet and let the kittens work up the courage to come out. The two kittens watched the room for a moment, their whiskers twitching. Then one of them padded out of the carrier – he was small enough that it was a big step down to the floor. He stumbled across the tiles to sniff at Amina's sandals.

"Mum!" Amina breathed, her eyes shining. "Look! He's tickling me!" She giggled and twitched, and the kitten play-pounced on the fabric flowers on her shoes. The second tabby kitten tumbled after the first one, eager to see what this exciting new game was.

James laughed and handed Amina a feathery toy. "Try this instead, otherwise your sandals might never be the same again." He smiled at Zara and offered her the basket of toys.

Zara took out a squishy toy fish and sat holding it, wondering if the kittens would come and investigate her too. But they were too interested in the feather wand that Amina was bouncing up and down. The two kittens looked like wind-up toys, turning their heads every time she wobbled the feathers. Mum and Dad and Amina were laughing delightedly, and Zara laughed too, even though she felt just a tiny bit jealous. She didn't want to take the kittens away from Amina – she only wished they'd play with her as well.

Then Zara glanced round, her attention caught by the smallest movement over by the carrier. Of course! There was another kitten! Zara had been so caught up watching the two tabby kittens that she'd forgotten about the little black-and-white girl. She was just stepping cautiously out of the carrier, trying to get down over the edge of the door.

Zara bit her lip as the kitten padded around with one paw, trying to work out how far down the floor was. She was definitely smaller than the tabbies and Zara was worried she might not be

able to get out. But eventually the kitten bumped down on to the tiles and stopped to look around again. Zara didn't know very much about cats – not yet – but she could tell the kitten wasn't nearly as confident and bouncy as her brother and sister. Maybe she was shy?

Zara was quite used to people talking about her as "the shy twin", or "the quiet one". People said it all the time, even though Mum and Dad tried to tell them not to. Only a couple of days ago, Dad had persuaded Amina to walk down to the shops with him, while Mum kept Zara behind to have a "little chat". Mum wanted to talk to her about the new school they were going to after the summer holidays, and about trying to make friends, and not letting Amina do all the talking. Zara had listened, of course she had, and nodded in all the right places and promised Mum she'd try. But it wasn't as easy as that. At their old school, Amina had done all the friend-making, and Zara didn't mind. It made things easier when Amina talked for her. Sometimes she did wish she had a best friend of her own though – as well as her twin, of course.

How do you make friends? Amina wondered as she watched the little black-and-white kitten tiptoe towards her. Perhaps it was just about being brave enough to go up to someone.

Holly Webb started out as a children's book editor and wrote her first series for the publisher she worked for. She has been writing ever since, with over one hundred books to her name. Holly lives in Berkshire, with her husband and three children. Holly's pet cats are always nosying around when she is trying to type on her laptop.

For more information about Holly Webb visit:

www.holly-webb.com